PAM JENOFF
THE
Ambassador's
Daughter

HARLEQUIN® MIRA®

Harlequin MIRA is a registered trademark of Harlequin Enterprises Limited, used under licence.

Published in Great Britain 2013
Harlequin MIRA, an imprint of Harlequin (UK) Limited,
Eton House, 18-24 Paradise Road,
Richmond, Surrey, TW9 1SR

© Pam Jenoff 2013

ISBN 978 1 848 45203 9

58-0213

Harlequin's policy is to use papers that are natural, renewable and recyclable products and made from wood grown in sustainable forests. The logging and manufacturing processes conform to the legal environmental regulations of the country of origin.

Printed and bound by CPI Group (UK) Ltd,
Croydon, CR0 4YY

Pam Jenoff is the author of several novels, including the international bestseller *Kommandant's Girl*, which also earned her a Quill Award nomination. Along with a bachelor degree in International Affairs from George Washington University and Master's degree in History from Cambridge, she received her *Juris Doctor* from the University of Pennsylvania and previously served as a Foreign Service Officer for the US State Department in Europe, as the Special Assistant to the Secretary of the Army at the Pentagon and as a practising attorney. Pam lives with her husband and three children near Philadelphia where, in addition to writing, she teaches law school.

In loving memory of Dad

THE
Ambassador's
Daughter

PROLOGUE

The sun has dropped low beneath the crumbling arches of Lehrter Bahnhof as I make my way across the station. A sharp, late-autumn breeze sends the pigeons fluttering from the rafters and I draw my coat closer against the chill. The crowds are sparse this Tuesday evening, the platforms bereft of the usual commuter trains and their disembarking passengers. A lone carriage sits on the track farthest to the right, silent and dark.

I had been surprised by the telegram announcing Stefan's return by rail. There were hardly any trains since the Allies had bombed the lines. At least that's what the newspapers write—the defunct trains and the British naval blockade are the excuses given for everything, from the lack of new pipes to start the water running again—a problem that has forced us back outside as though it were a century ago—to the impossibility of getting fresh milk. Looking around the desolate station now, I almost believe the excuse.

Stefan's face appears in my mind. It was more than four years ago on this very platform that we said goodbye, the garland of asters I'd picked hung freshly around his neck. "Don't go," I pleaded a final time. Stefan was not cut out to fight—he had a round, gentle face, wide brown eyes that said he could never hurt anybody. But it was too late—he had gone down to the enlistment center two weeks earlier, ahead of any conscription, and come home with papers ordering him to report. The war was going to be quick, everyone said. The horse-mounted Serbs, with their swords, were no match for the Kaiser's tanks and planes. The fighting would be over in weeks, and all of the boys wanted a piece of the glory before it was gone.

I peer back over my shoulder past the closing kiosk, which gives off the smell of stale ersatz coffee, at the station doors, creaking open and closed with the wind. Someone more important than me should have been here to meet Stefan. He is a soldier, wounded in battle. More to the point, he is the only young man from our Jewish enclave in Berlin who had gone off to fight and come back at all. I don't know what I expected, not a marching band and reporters exactly, but perhaps a small delegation from the local war council. The once-proud veterans' group had been disbanded, though. No one wanted to be identified as a soldier now, to face the glares of reproach and the questions about why they had not gotten the job done.

Fifteen minutes pass, then twenty. I clutch tighter the fine leather gloves that I've managed to twist into a damp, wrinkled ball. Fighting the urge to pace, I start toward the station office to inquire if there is news of the next arrival. I navigate around a luggage trolley, which has been upended and abandoned midstation. My skirt catches on something and I pause, turning to free the hem. It is not a nail or board, but a filthy, long-haired man sitting on the ground, a fetid mass of bandages where his right leg had once been.

"*Bitte…*" a voice rasps as I jump backward. "I'm sorry to startle you." He is a soldier, too, or was, his tattered uniform barely recognizable. I fish a coin from my purse, trying not to recoil from the hand that reaches out for it. But inwardly, I blanch. Will Stefan look like this sorry creature?

I lift my head as a horn sounds long and low from the darkness beyond the edge of the station. A moment later a train appears, threading its way onto one of the tracks. It moves so slowly that it seems to have no engine at all, nudged instead by some slight tilt of the earth. Great clouds of steam billow from its funnel, filling the station. As I walk toward the platform, straining to see through the mist, my heart begins to pound.

The train grinds to a halt. The doors open with painstaking slowness and a few men spill out, some in uniform and others street clothes. I search those walking toward me for Stefan, knowing that he will not be among them.

When the platform has nearly cleared, a nurse pushes a wheelchair from one of the train carriages. I step forward, and then stop again. The chair does not contain Stefan, but an elderly man, hunched over so only the top of his bald head shows. The nurse struggles with the chair and as its rear wheels catch on the door, I hasten to help her.

The man in the chair uncurls, straightening slightly as I near. It is Stefan, I realize, biting my lip so hard I taste blood. A giant slash across the right side of his face from temple to chin combines with the lack of hair to make him almost unrecognizable. But the worst part is his arms, skeletal and shaky. My mind races as I try to fathom the horrors that could age a man decades in a few years.

Stefan gazes up with vacant, watery eyes, not speaking. "Hello, darling," I manage, bending to brush my lips against his papery cheek.

He reaches for me with a quivering hand. "Let's go home," he croaks, and as his fingers close around my wrist like cold death, I let out the cry I can hold back no longer.

My eyes fly open and I sit up in the darkness, still screaming.

PART ONE

Paris, December 1918

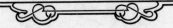

1

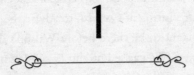

I cycle through the Jardin des Tuileries, navigating carefully around the slippery spots on the damp gravel path. The December air is crisp with the promise of snow and the bare branches of the chestnut trees bow over me like a procession of sabers. I pedal faster past the park benches, savoring the wind against my face and opening my mouth to gulp the air. A startled squirrel darts behind the base of a marble statute. My hair loosens, a sail billowing behind me, pushing me farther and faster, and for a moment it is almost possible to forget that I am in Paris.

The decision to come had not been mine. "I've been asked to go to the peace conference," Papa informed me unexpectedly less than a month ago. He had previously professed no interest in taking part in "the dog and pony show at Versailles," and had harrumphed frequently as he read the details of the preparations in the *Times*. "Uncle Walter thinks…" he added, as he so often did. I did not need to listen to the rest. My mother's older brother, an industrialist who had taken over the electronics firm their father founded, could not attend the peace conference himself after contributing so much to the war machine. He considered it important, though, to somehow have a voice at the table, a presence before the Germans were formally summoned. So he had secured an invitation for Papa, an academic who had spent the war visiting at Oxford, to advise the conference. It was important to be there before Wilson's ship arrived, Papa explained. We packed up our leased town house hurriedly and boarded a ferry at Dover.

Papa had not been happy to come, either, I reflect, as I reach the end of the park and slow. The street is choked thick with motorcars and lorries and autobuses, and a few terrified horses trying to pull carriages amid the traffic. He had pulled forlornly on his beard as we boarded the train in Calais, bound for Paris. It was not just his reluctance to be torn from his studies at the university, immersed in the research and teaching he loved so, and thrust into the glaring spotlight of the world's political stage. We are the defeated, a vanquished people, and in the French capital we loved before the war, we are now regarded as the enemy. In England, it had been bad enough. Though Papa's academic status prevented him from being interned like so many German men, we were outsiders, eyed suspiciously at the university. I could not wear the war ribbon as the smug British girls did when their fiancés were off fighting, because mine was for the wrong side. But outside of our immediate Oxford circle it had been relatively easy to fade into the crowd with my accentless English. Here, people know who we are, or will, once the conference formally begins. The recriminations will surely be everywhere.

My skirts swish airily as I climb from the bike, thankfully free of the crinolines that used to make riding so cumbersome. The buildings on the rue Cambon sparkle, their shrapnel-pocked facades washed fresh by the snow. I stare up at the endless apartments, stacked on top of one another, marveling at the closeness of it all, unrivaled by the most crowded quarters in London. How do they live in such spaces? Sometimes I feel as though I am suffocating just looking at them. Growing up in Berlin, I'm no stranger to cities. But everything here is exponentially bigger—the wide, traffic-clogged boulevards, square after square grander than the next. The pavement is packed, too, with lines of would-be customers beneath the low striped awning of the cheese shop, and outside the chocolatier where the sign says a limited quantity will be available at three o'clock. A warm, delicious aroma portends the sweets' arrival.

A moment later, I turn onto a side street and pull the bike up against the wall, which is covered in faded posters exhorting passersby to buy war bonds. A bell tinkles as I enter the tiny bookshop. *"Bonjour."* The owner, Monsieur Batteau, accustomed to my frequent visits, nods but does not look up from the till.

I squeeze down one of the narrow aisles and scan the packed shelves hungrily. When we first arrived in Paris weeks earlier, it was books that I missed the most: the dusty stacks of the college library at Magdalen, the bounty of the stalls at the Portobello Road market. Then one day I happened upon this shop. Books had become a luxury few Parisians could afford during the war and there were horrible stories of people burning them for kindling, or using their pages for toilet paper. But some had instead brought them to places like this, selling them for a few francs in order to buy bread. The result is a shop bursting at the seams with books, piled haphazardly in floor-to-ceiling stacks ready to topple over at any moment. I run my hand over a dry, cracked binding with affection. The titles are odd—old storybooks mix with volumes about politics and poetry in a half-dozen languages and an abundance of war novels, for which it seems no one has the stomach anymore.

I hold up a volume of Goethe. It has to be at least a hundred years old, but other than its yellowed pages it is in good condition, its spine still largely intact. Before the war, it would have been worth money. Here, it sits discarded and unrecognized, a gem among the rubble.

"*Pardon,*" Monsieur Batteau says a short while later, "but if you'd like to buy anything…" I glance up from the travelogue of Africa I'd been browsing. I've been in the shop scarcely thirty minutes and the light outside has not yet begun to fade. "I'm closing early today, on account of the parade."

"Of course." How could I have forgotten? President Wilson arrives today. I stand and pass Monsieur Batteau a few coins, then tuck the Goethe tome and the book on botany I'd selected into my satchel. Outside the street is transformed—the queues have dissipated, replaced with soldiers and men in tall hats and women with parasols, all moving in a singular direction. Leaving the bike, I allow myself to be carried by the stream as it feeds into the rue de Rivoli. The wide boulevard, now closed to motorcars, is filled with pedestrians.

The movement of the crowd stops abruptly. A moment later we surge forward again, reaching the massive octagon of the Place de la Concorde, the mottled gray buildings stately and resplendent in the late-afternoon sun. The storied square where Marie Antoinette and Louis XVI were executed is an endless mass of bodies, punctuated by the captured German cannons brought here after the armistice. The statues in the corners, each symbolizing a French town, have been covered in laurels.

The crowd pushes in behind me, onlookers from every side street attempting to pack the already choked space. I am surrounded by a sea of tall men, the damp wool from their coats pressing against my face, making it impossible to breathe. Close spaces have never suited me. Trying not to panic, I squeeze through to one of the cannons. I hitch my skirt and climb onto the wheel, the steel icy against my legs through my stockings. *"Pardon,"* I say to the startled young man already on top of the gun.

There are flags everywhere, I can see from my new vantage point, banners unfurled from the balconies of the columned Hôtel de Crillon, American flags in the hands of the children. "Wilson the Just!" placards declare. A lane has been formed through the square, roped off with great swaths of sky-blue cloth to keep the crowd back. Airplanes, lower and louder than I've ever heard, roar overhead.

A few feet to the right of the cannon, a woman in a blue cape catches my eye. Nearly forty by the looks of her, she stands still in the feverish crowd. She is tall, her posture perfectly erect, with chestnut-brown hair piled upon her head. She is somehow familiar, though from where I cannot say. Abruptly, she turns and begins walking, swimming against the tide, slipping away from the gathering. Who would leave before Wilson's arrival? Surely there is nowhere else to be in the city now. I wonder fleetingly if she is ill, but her movements are calm and fluid as she disappears into the crowd.

The din grows to a roar. I turn my attention back to the square as a row of mounted soldiers canters into view, wearing the bright helmets of the Garde Republicaine. The horses raise their heads high, snorting great clouds of frost from their flared nostrils. The crowd pushes in, twisting the once-straight lane into a serpentine. I shudder as unseen guns erupt jarringly in the distance. Surely that is not a sound any of us needs to hear anymore.

Behind the horses, a procession of open carriages appears. The first bears a man in a long coat and top hat with a woman beside him. Though it is too far away for me to see, I can tell by the whoops that he is President Wilson. As the carriage draws closer and stops in front of the hotel, I recognize Wilson from the photos. He waves to the crowd as he climbs down. But his bespectacled face is solemn, as if seeing for the first time the hopes of so many that hang on his promises.

A minute later Wilson disappears into the hotel. The show quickly over, the onlookers begin to ebb, bleeding down the dozen or so arteries that lead from the square. I glimpse the woman in the blue cape, several yards away now, still fighting her way through the crowd. Impulsively, I hop down from the cannon, catching the hem of my skirt as I do. I free the material, then push toward her, weaving through narrow gaps, heedless now of the closeness as I follow the flash of blue like a beacon.

As I reach the street, I spy the woman fifty or so meters ahead, turning into the park where I'd been cycling an hour earlier. There is nothing unusual about that. But one would not have left Wilson's arrival for a stroll and her gait is purposeful, suggesting an errand more interesting than just fresh air. I push forward, following her into the park. A moment later, she turns off the main path into a smaller garden where I've not been before.

I pause. A gate, tall and tarnished, marks the entrance, elaborate lions carved into either side standing sentry. Ahead, the path is obscured by winter brush. *Turn back,* a voice seems to say. But the woman in blue has disappeared at a turn in the bend and I cannot resist following her.

I step through the gate and into the garden. A few meters farther, the path ends at a small, frozen pond, dividing to follow its banks on either side. I scan the deserted park benches, but do not see the woman. From beyond the bend comes the sound of laughter. I follow the path as it curves around the pond and it opens to reveal a wide expanse of frozen water, nestled in a cove of trees. A group of well-dressed young women in their late teens, perhaps a year or two younger than me, skate on the ice, chatting in loud, carefree voices.

Across the pond, something stirs against one of the trees. The woman in blue. Will she join the skaters? Maybe two decades older, she appears an odd fit, but the conference has brought together all sorts of unusual people, blurring the conventions and distinctions that might have separated them back home. The woman hangs in the shadows, like the witch out of a fairy tale, watching the skaters raptly. Her gaze is protective and observant, a scientist studying a subject about which she really cares.

The skaters start for the bank and the woman in blue steps back, disappearing. I consider following her farther, but the sun has dropped low behind the trees, the early winter afternoon fading.

Twenty minutes later, having retrieved my bike, I reach the hotel. Papa chose our lodgings at the tiny Hôtel Relais Saint-Honoré carefully. Just across the river from the foreign ministry, it keeps him close to the conference proceedings while still maintaining a bit of privacy. The lobby, with its cluster of red velvet chairs in the corner, feels more like a parlor.

"Mademoiselle," the desk clerk calls as I cross the lobby. I turn back reluctantly. He holds out a letter toward me, between his thumb and forefinger, as though the German postmark might somehow be infected. I reach for it, my stomach sinking as I eye the wobbly script.

I start for the elevator once more. As the doors open, I am confronted unexpectedly by Papa and two men with swarthy complexions and dark mustaches. "And if you look at the prewar boundaries…" Papa, speaking in French, stops midsentence as he sees me. "Hello, darling. Gentlemen, may I present my daughter? Margot, these are Signore DiVincenzo and Ricci of the Italian delegation."

"A pleasure," I say. They nod and stare at me strangely. It is my dress, soiled and torn at the hem from where I caught it on the cannon, as well as my disheveled hair. I may quite possibly smell, too, from my vigorous bike ride through the park.

But Papa does not seem to notice, just smiles a warm mix of affection and pride. "I'll be up in a moment, my dear." It is not just that he is an absentminded academic—Papa has always accepted me wholly as I am, with all of my rough spots and imperfections. He is not bothered by my unkempt appearance, any more than I mind his predisposition to forgetting about meals or the days of the week.

The attendant closes the elevator gates and my stomach flutters in the queer way it always does as we ride upward to the third floor. I unlock the door to our suite, which consists of a bedroom each for Papa and me, adjoined by a sitting room. I go to the washroom and run the water in the large, claw-foot tub, then pour in some salts. As the tub fills, I remove my soiled dress and the undergarments that have etched themselves to my body. Crinolines may have gone out of style but corsets, unfortunately, are another matter. I turn off the tap and slip into the deep, warm bath, grateful to be enveloped by the steam.

Thinking of the unopened letter, Stefan's face appears. It is hard to remember exactly when we became romantically involved. He had always been present—a boy on the neighboring block and in the class a grade above mine across the hallway at school. We had played together often as children and he'd been beside me at my mother's funeral, taking my hand and helping me slip away from the crowded house after. One autumn morning when I was fifteen and reading on the front step of our home in Berlin, Stefan rode by on his bicycle, slowing but not quite stopping as he passed.

This did not strike me as unusual—he had a paper route delivering the *Post* to the houses on our block that ordered it. Half an hour passed and he circled again. I looked up, my curiosity piqued. Stefan's house was around the corner on a nicer block than ours, twice as big but with a drooping roof and cracked steps in need of repair. I'd seen him on our street three or more times a day lately, though the paper came only daily.

"Wait," I called after him, standing up. He stopped abruptly, grabbing the handlebar to stop the bike from lurching sideways. "Did you want something?"

He climbed off the bike and set it down at the curb then walked over to me. There was something different about him. Though his strawberry-blond hair and pale skin were the same, he had started shaving, the peach fuzz that had once adorned his upper lip now a faint stubble. He had shot up in height and stood several inches above me and there was a new thickness to his arms.

"I was wondering," he said, "if you'd like to go to the movies."

I averted my eyes, caught off guard. I'd expected an invitation to join the football game the boys played Sundays in the park, though Tante Celia said I was getting too old for such things. But his tone was different now and when I turned back to him, I noticed that perspiration soaked his collar. He was nervous.

"Yes," I say hurriedly, wanting to ease his discomfort.

"I'll call for you tonight at seven." He stepped backward, nearly tripping over his bike before getting on and racing away.

The night at the movies was unremarkable, an American comedy, followed by an ice cream at the Eiscafé. After that day, Stefan became increasingly present, coming by the house after school, joining us for Sunday lunch at Uncle Walter's villa in Grunewald. One afternoon as we strolled around the lake behind the villa, I looked down at our hands, fingers intertwined, and realized that we were courting. Not that it was so very different from when we had just been friends. Stefan was unobtrusive and left me to my own devices. Being with him was rather like being with myself.

We were at Uncle Walter's for Sunday lunch when news of the war came. One of his aides rushed into the dining room and whispered in his ear and he broke the usual quiet by turning on the radio that sat on the mantelpiece. The men nodded with approval as Germany's declaration of war crackled over the airwaves. Our ally Austria's Archduke Franz Ferdinand had been assassinated, murdered in broad daylight by a heathen Serb. We had to take a stand.

Ten minutes later, I climb from the tub, still thinking of Stefan as I dry and put on a fresh dress. I could have gone back to Berlin after the war, insisted that Papa allow me to be with Stefan as he recovers. But I had not. I swallow against my guilt. He is well cared for by his family. It is me he wants above all else, though, I can tell from his letters, which always speak excitedly of my return. I have sent packages of French jellies and other delicacies, but answering his letters is harder. What can I say to this man I hardly know anymore?

I rummage through my toiletries for some salve to relieve my hands, which have grown dry and chapped from the air here. It is my insistence on taking off my gloves too often, Tante Celia says. The items in my kit are few—some face powder, a single tube of pale pink lipstick for special occasions, a fragrance that Celia had given me for my birthday last year, too flowery for my taste.

By the time I emerge, Papa has returned, shuffling papers at the rolltop desk in the corner that doubles as his study over a glass of Pernod. Dinner, two plates covered by metal domes and a thick loaf of bread wrapped in cloth, sits unserved as is our preference.

"Papa," I say gently, nudging him from his work. I bring the candlesticks down from the mantelpiece as he pours the wine. *"Baruch atah Adonai…"*

"Celia is at a reception," he says without my asking when we've finished the blessings. I exhale slightly. I would not have been uncharitable and turned away kin with nowhere to go. But spending each Sabbath together is a tradition that Papa and I have observed wherever we have been in the world, bringing our silver Kiddush cup and candlesticks with us, and we continue it here in Paris. No matter how busy he is, Papa always stops what he is doing so that we can have a meal and talk, just the two of us.

I cut the crusty, still-warm loaf of bread. Living in the hotel, it is easy to forget about the shortages the outside world still endures. I hand Papa a piece and notice then that his face is pale. Though he is immaculately dressed and groomed as always, a trim sliver of silver hair circling his head, there are dark circles around his eyes. "Have you taken your medicine?" I ask gently. He gets so caught up in his work that he can forget to eat or sleep much less to take the pills that the doctor said are important for his heart condition. I've been reminding him for as long as I can remember.

Before he can answer, I sneeze once, then again. "It's the dry air," I say hastily, reaching for my handkerchief. Papa's brow wrinkles with consternation, now his turn to worry about me. Spanish flu, like the one that had taken my mother more than a decade ago, has been on the rise since autumn. Though I had also come down with the flu as a child, it had spared me like the angel of death in the Passover story, passing by as if lamb's blood had been painted on the door. I had labored with a fever for days. Then I'd awakened with a permanent crescent-shaped scar on my neck, a reaction to one of the medicines.

But this new flu strain is even more virulent, having taken twelve lives at Oxford alone before our departure. People talked endlessly about how to prevent it—wash out the nose with warm water and soda, wear garlic around the neck, drink a shot of whiskey before bedtime. Some whispered that the Germans unleashed it as a weapon of war, stopping just short of blaming me and Papa personally. "More likely," Papa said once, "it came across the Atlantic with the soldiers." In London, people had all but stopped going out. But here the parties continue on gaily, as if germs were some invention of the science fiction writers.

I sample a spoonful of the rich coq au vin. "I'm fine, really. Tell me about your day."

As we eat, Papa describes his meeting with the men

from the Italian delegation, who are seeking his support for an independent Macedonia. "And then there are the West African colonies," he says, jumping topics as always with mercurial speed. "The French are going to put up a fight on granting independence. They want mandates instead."

"So it is only to be self-determination for some."

"*Liebchen,* we must be practical. One cannot change the entire world in just a few months."

Then what is the point of the conference? I wonder. "We have to work within the system," he adds, as if responding to my unspoken question. "Though I know you do not agree. Enough about my work," he says, as I clear the plates and set out coffee and apple cake. "How are you, my dear?"

"Fine. A bit restless."

"Oh? I thought you and Celia might enjoy some of the museums...." His voice trails off and he winces at the gulf between me and mother's sister, a woman he dearly wishes I would accept. "Perhaps if you had a brother or sister," he frets, as he has so many times over the years. Small families like ours are the exception rather than the rule but, for some reason not quite clear to me, siblings had not been possible.

I kiss his cheek. "I would not have cared to share you," I say, trying to assuage his guilt. It is the truth. The two of us have always been enough. I see then our Sabbath meals as a tableau, a scene that has played itself out in various cities over the years. "And I'm fine, really. The parties are all well and good, but the women are just silly." I stop, hearing myself complaining again.

"Would you be happier outside the city?" Papa asks.

I contemplate the question. I have always felt freest when close to nature, like on the hiking trips we took when I was a child. Papa, despite being bookish, had an amazing capacity for the outdoors, an ability to navigate the densest forest without a compass, to find fresh water and sense the weather that was coming. We would climb high with a day's food in our packs and stay in the cabins that populated the high hills, reaching the next before sundown.

But Paris, while cramped, has a certain energy. And I don't want to be exiled to some boring suburb with Tante Celia. "I don't know. I don't think so, anyway."

It isn't the city itself that I dislike, I decide as we eat dessert. I came here every spring as a child, shopping the fine boutiques of Faubourg Saint-Honoré with my mother until Papa joined us at the end of the day for cakes at one of the patisseries. I'd even dreamed of one day studying at the Sorbonne.

No, it's Paris *now* that I hate. On the eve of the conference, the city is bursting at the seams with journalists and delegates from every conceivable cause and country. Hotels empty since before the war have been aired out, their rooms hastily refreshed to accommodate everyone who has come to the show. I don't mind those who have cause to be here, the stuffy clusters of suited men who will decide the future of the world, the scrappy delegates from countries seeking to be born. But the hangers-on, the socialites and doyennes that have come to provide the parties and other window dressing, having stifled Paris to the choking point.

"Well, the question will be out of our hands at some point. When the Germans arrive," he says. My brow wrinkles. We *are* the Germans. "The official delegation, I mean, we'll be expected to go out to Versailles where they are to be housed."

I consider this new bit of information. The conference proceedings are being held in Paris, but the Germans will be housed outside in Versailles. The site where the Germans had imposed their draconian peace terms on France a half-century earlier, it is now where we are to get our just deserts. "Are the conference proceedings to move out there when the delegation arrives?"

"Not that I'm aware."

"But one would think, if the Germans are to participate in the conference that they should be near the meetings...."

"One would think." He pauses for a sip of coffee. "One would think that they would have invited the German delegation here for the early months of the conference if they were really to participate."

How could one negotiate peace without the other side at the table? "Are you familiar with the delegation?" I ask.

"Oh, the usual sorts. Rantzau—he's the new foreign minister—as well as the defense minister and the ambassador, of course, Uncle Walter's old nemesis." The men in power form a very tight club, raised in the same circles and educated at the same schools. It was a club to which Papa had never wanted to belong, but now he had found himself drawn back in by the conference. "There's a younger fellow, too, a military captain, but I can't recall his name."

"Are they bringing anyone with them? Families, I mean?"

Papa shakes his head. "Hotel accommodations are quite limited in Versailles." It was unusual for delegates, even from the victorious countries, to bring their wives and children. "You still haven't told me what you've been up to today, other than avoiding Tante Celia."

I consider mentioning the woman in the blue cape, but even in my head it sounds inconsequential, my own interest silly. "I saw Wilson's arrival today," I say instead.

"Oh?"

"The crowd was most receptive."

"They have such high hopes. The Fourteen Points, self-determination, a new world order..." He shakes his head. "Wilson is idealistic. It's like the notion in Judaism—*tikun olam* means, quite literally, to repair the world. That's what he is trying to do."

"You don't think he will be able to do it."

"I think it isn't that simple." He picks up his pipe, but does not light it, instead waving it like a pointer in a lecture hall. "Take self-determination for example. What does that mean? Who is the self—a nationality, a religious group or something altogether different?" He jabs at the air in front of him. "Do I believe they will make a difference or reshape the world? I don't know. The world will never go back to what it was—kaisers and czars and kings, but the question is whether we can make something better in its place. I believe the world will be a better place for the trying." He sighs. "Anyway, you'll get to see a bit more of Wilson at the welcoming reception tomorrow night." I cock my head. "I mentioned it to you last week." The social calendar had been so full with stuffy affairs, I'd stopped listening, rather allowing Papa and Celia to lead me where needed. "It should be quite the occasion."

I groan. "Must I attend?"

"I'm afraid so. It is an important event and it wouldn't do for us to miss it. You've heard from Stefan?" he asks, changing the subject again. Papa has allowed me much liberty as a young woman, but on this one point he pushes. He is nearly seventy now, and eager to see me settled, rather than left alone in the world.

"I have." I do not admit that I've not opened today's letter, instead focusing on things that Stefan wrote last week. "They've apparently got a good deal of snow in Berlin, much more so than here."

He nods. "Uncle Walter said the same. I'm sure you are eager to return to him. Stefan that is, not Uncle Walter." I smile at this. My mother's brother has never been a favorite of mine. "How is he?" Papa asks, an unmistakable note of fondness to his voice. Papa always liked Stefan—their gentle personalities were well suited to each other. Stefan did not share Papa's razor-sharp intellect, but he always listened with rapt attention to Papa talk about the latest article he was writing.

"He's working very hard at rehabilitation. He's even managed to stand up a few times."

"That's remarkable. He wasn't expected to live, so to get out of a chair is really something. Perhaps he'll even get around with a walker someday. What an extraordinary young man."

A pang of jealousy shoots through me. In some ways, Stefan is the son Papa never had. Not that Stefan could follow Papa into academia. The Osters were a once well-to-do banking family that had fallen on hard times. Stefan, as the oldest of four children and the only son, has been expected to somehow restore the family to a better station. We had hoped that he might join Uncle Walter and run one of the plants. But imagining him trying to navigate around the heavy machinery of the factory floor with a walker seems quite impossible now.

"He is doing really well," I say, but something nags at me. "Do you think he is damaged, beyond his legs, I mean? His letters just feel a little off." Papa wrinkles his brow, as if asking me to say more. But I can't quite articulate my concern.

"It's the war, darling. Give him time." I nod. Stefan is such a good man. My heart breaks for the things he has seen and suffered. I cannot help but wonder, though, whether he will ever be whole again.

"Hopefully the conference will move quickly and we can return to Berlin soon so you can see him."

I swallow over the lump that has formed in my throat. "Hopefully."

"Good night, dear." He walks to the desk and reaches for a stack of papers. Despite his slight size and quiet demeanor, Papa has always been the strongest man I've known. Not just strong: brave. Once when I was about six we'd been walking our German shepherd, Gunther, through the Tiergarten when a large stray confronted us, blocking the path ahead. My first instinct had been to leap back in fear. But Papa moved forward placing himself between gentle Gunther and the snarling beast. In that moment, I understood what it took to be a parent, in a way I might never quite be able to manage myself.

He has given up so much to raise me. After Mother died,

it would have been logical for him to leave my upbringing to Tante Celia or governesses. But instead he had cut short his schedule at the university, declining to teach in the late afternoon and evening, and taking his work home so he could read alongside me. He had made me a part of his journeys and declined the opportunities where he could not because the destinations were too far-flung or the travel unsafe or good schools not available. There were times, I could tell, that conversation was too much and he was eager to escape into his work from the harshness of everyday life and the pain that he carried. He made sure, though, that I was never alone.

But now, hunched over the desk, he appears vulnerable. I am seized with the urge to reach down and hug him. Instead, I place a hand on his shoulder. He looks up, startled by my unexpected touch. We have never been very physically affectionate. "Good night, Papa."

I return the dinner tray to the hall, then carry the lamp to my room so that Papa can work in the sitting room uninterrupted. I pull out the volume of Goethe I'd purchased from the bookseller and run my hand over the cover. Stefan would love it—or would have, once upon a time. We had always shared a deep passion for books and our families were frequently amused to find us sitting together under a tree in the garden or in the parlor, reading silently side by side, each lost in our own world. But is he even reading now? And would the book, with its references to death and suffering, just make things worse for him? I set it down on the table.

Stefan's letter sits on the dresser. Reluctantly I open it.

Dearest Margot—

I can tell from the almost illegible script that he has tried to write himself this time instead of having the nurse do it.

I hope that this letter finds you well. Exciting news: Father is modifying the cottage and building an extension for us so we can live there after the wedding.

I cringe. Stefan is immobilized in a wheelchair—of course he cannot return to the Berlin town house with its many narrow stairs. I recall the Osters' vacation cottage, a two-room house on the edge of a maudlin lake, more than an hour from the city. Are we really to live in the middle of nowhere? How will he earn a living?

I finger the ring that Stefan gave me before leaving for the front. I should have gone to be with him, a voice inside me nags for the hundredth time. I had good reasons for not going—first the war and later the railway lines and now Papa being summoned to Paris. There were ways I might have gone, though, if I pushed hard enough. But I hadn't, instead embracing the excuses like a mantle, shielding myself from the truth that inevitably awaits. I slip the ring from my finger and put it in my pocket.

I fold the letter and put it back into the envelope without reading further.

A scrap of paper falls from the envelope and flutters to the floor. A photograph. I pick it up, wishing he had not sent it. He meant it as a good thing, sitting up in the wheelchair and smiling as if to say, *Look how far I've come.* In some ways it is better than the man I see in my nightmares, but his face is a stranger's to me, the hollow eyes confirming everything I fear about our future together.

Perhaps being in Paris is not the worst thing, after all.

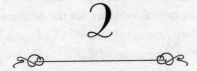

2

As we ascend the marble staircase to the ballroom at the Hôtel de Crillon, my impression is one of white—wreaths of lilies and roses climbing the columns, great swaths of snowy tulle draped from the balconies above. "I'll just be a moment," Papa says, heading in the direction of the cloakroom with our coats. I take the glass of wine that is offered to me by one of the servers, then step out of the flow of the crowd. The reception is like all of the other parties we have attended since coming to Paris, only magnified tenfold, the pond of gray-haired men in black tuxedos now a sea. A handful of women in expensive gowns, the deep maroon and dusky-rose shades that are the fashion this year, cling to the periphery. The savory smell of the hors d'oeuvres mixes with a cacophony of floral perfumes and cigarette smoke.

The orchestra at the front of the room breaks from the waltz it had been playing midstanza and bursts into a robust rendition of "The Star-Spangled Banner." The guests hush, turning expectantly toward the entrance and there is a low murmur as President and Mrs. Wilson enter. The crowd parts to let them through. Closer now, he is taller than I thought, with a grimly set jaw.

A man I recognize from other occasions as the American ambassador, Stan Stahl, steps forward to greet the Wilsons. But before he can reach them, an Oriental boy, no older than myself, cuts in front of him and approaches the president. The boy, who wears not the uniform of a formal server but the white shirt and apron of the kitchen staff, holds an envelope outstretched in his shaking hand. An audible gasp runs through the ballroom.

One of the guards flanking Wilson moves to place himself between the president and the boy, but Wilson shakes him off. "He means no harm." Wilson takes the letter and opens it. "Thank you," he says, as solemnly as though he is speaking with one of the other Allied leaders. Apparently satisfied, the kitchen boy bows, then turns and disappears through one of the servers' doors. Yelling can be heard from the other side.

What does the letter say, I wonder. The spectacle over, the crowd closes in to greet the Wilsons. I scan the room for Papa and find him in the corner, shanghaied by someone, undoubtedly a delegate wanting to secure his support for a resolution. Now that the conference is about to begin in earnest, those lobbying for certain issues have dropped all pretense of subtlety, haranguing Papa and others in positions of influence nonstop for their support. I don't mind his being delayed—it is easier to be anonymous on my own, to slip back among the draperies and observe rather than participate. I only hope he will be able to extricate himself at some point. My curiosity at seeing Wilson satisfied, I am eager to escape back to the hotel, out of this starchy gown that Tante Celia selected for me and back to the novel I'd been reading.

The orchestra begins playing a waltz. Watching couples swirl around the floor, a memory flashes through my mind of a night not long after Stefan and I had started courting when he had come to the house to escort me to a school dance. He had arrived too early and as I brushed my hair I could hear him talking with Papa in the parlor below, their conversation somehow more awkward than usual. I came downstairs a few minutes later and Stefan's eyes widened at the sight of me in my pink party dress. His hair was freshly trimmed and he wore a crisp white shirt I had not seen before.

"Here." He held out a small corsage. As he helped me pin it on awkwardly, I smelled the aftershave he had surely borrowed from his father. We did not speak on the short ride to school. Everything was more formal, the way he held doors for me and helped me from the car, and I disliked the stiffness that interfered with our usual easy company. The school cafeteria had been decorated with crepe paper and vases of fresh wildflowers that could not quite mask the lingering smell of sauerkraut and wurst lunches that had worn its way into the cinder-block walls over the years.

As I see Stefan's face in my mind, an unexpected flash of tenderness wells up inside me. He cared for me in a way that no one ever had except Papa—and I liked that. Before him, my world had always been solitary, with my mother gone and Papa ensconced in his work. Stefan's near-constant presence made me feel somehow less alone. But I am longing for the boy I left four years ago. Even if I returned to Berlin this minute, things would be different.

My foot throbs, reminding me of the cracked dress shoe

that I've neglected for months to replace. I duck into one of the side salons off the main ballroom, where a handful of people cluster around small tables with tiny white candles at the center, and sink into an empty chair by a potted fern. In the far corner, an older woman sits at a piano, head bowed, eyes closed as she plays.

When the pianist lifts her head I gasp slightly. She is the woman in blue who fled Wilson's arrival, the one I'd followed from the square. That is why she looked familiar—I have seen her playing at a handful of the other gatherings since we arrived. I stand and start toward the piano. She is not beautiful, I decide instantly. The bridge of her nose is curved and her eyes set close, giving her a hawkish appearance. But her cheekbones are high and her hair upswept, making the harsh somehow regal.

I watch, fascinated. It is unusual to see a female musician, or a woman doing anything other than accompanying a man on his arm at these affairs. Of course, there are the cooks and maids and such, but the woman's high-collared silk blouse and straight posture does not bespeak the serving class. She plays with her whole body, shoulders swaying side to side as her hands traverse the keys, partners in a dance.

She finishes playing and the last note resonates throughout the salon, but the guests are too engrossed in their conversations to notice or applaud. "That was lovely," I remark. The woman glances up and I wait for her to thank me, or at least smile. But a flicker of something close to annoyance crosses her face. "Mahler, wasn't it?" I say.

She blinks. "Yes, from his *Sixth Symphony*." Her voice is low and husky, just short of masculine, and her French is accented slightly, hailing from somewhere eastern I cannot place.

"One of my favorites, though I haven't heard it since before the war. I didn't think they would have you play it here." My words come out more bluntly that I'd intended.

"Music is not political."

I want to tell her that everything is political now, from the wine that is served (always the chardonnay, never the Riesling) to the color of the tablecloths (a patriotic French blue). But I do not know her well enough to get into a debate.

"I play what I want," the woman adds. She adjusts the thick chignon of hair, the chestnut color broken by a few strands of gray. "It's not as if they pay me."

"Oh?"

The woman shakes her head. "My parents won't allow it. They think it would be unseemly to take money." It sounds odd, a woman who must be close to forty listening to her parents. But I will always care about Papa's approval.

She points through the doorway toward a cluster of silver-haired men in the main ballroom. "My father. He's a diplomat."

"Mine, as well." I leap too eagerly at the commonality, ignoring the fact that Papa's title is in fact only a formality, conferred to credential him to the conference.

"Mine is with the Polish delegation." My excitement fades. The Germans and Poles had been on opposite sides of the war, enemies. We could not, in fact, have less in common. "I'm Polish, or will be if they ever get around to making us a country again," she adds. I nod. Poland had been partitioned among Germany, Austria and Russia for the better part of a half century. "Hard to see how they'll have the time with all of this socializing." She gestures toward the larger gathering. "You're German, aren't you?"

I flush. I had worked so hard to remove any trace of an accent from both my French and English. But a musician with a trained ear, the woman can hear the slight flaws in my speech and discern their origin. "Yes." I hold my breath, waiting some sign of disapproval.

Her expression remains neutral. "Or at least you are until they get around to making Germany no longer a country," she says wryly.

I cringe at this. It is the great unanswered question of the peace conference, whispered about in the salons, debated openly in the bars and parties: What will happen to Germany? "Back home they believe that it will be a fair peace."

"Yes, they have to, don't they? I'm Krysia Smok," she says, extending a hand.

"Margot Rosenthal. A pleasure." I want to mention the fact that I have seen her before but that would beg the question of what she was doing in the park, too intrusive of someone I've just met.

"I didn't think the German delegation was coming until late spring," she remarks.

"They aren't. That is, we aren't part of the delegation. My father is a professor, he teaches at Oxford at the moment...." I can hear myself babbling now. "And he's detailed to the conference, not the delegation." I study her face, wondering if she is impressed by the distinction.

From behind the column comes tittering laughter. "Really, even the kitchen staff have political aims," a woman comments in English. "Are we to have soufflé tonight or a political rally?"

"They say the Japanese will demand a statement of racial equality, too," her companion replies in a hushed tone, as though saying it aloud might make it real.

"Americans," Krysia scoffs as they walk away. "They think they're so progressive. And yet women in the States still do not have the right to vote." I consider her point. Women were only given the vote in Germany a year ago and I haven't been back to have the chance.

Papa is at my side then. "Darling, I'm sorry to have left you. I was waylaid by a Dutchman."

"It's quite fine. Did you hear about the kitchen boy?"

"Yes, Indochinese, by the sound of things, and seeking Wilson's support for some sort of autonomy."

"Do you think he lost his job?"

"I think," Papa replies gently, "that he did what he set out to do at the conference and…" He stops midsentence and turns to Krysia. "Forgive my manners." Papa is not like some of the men at the conference, seeing through the staff as though they are not here. "I'm Margot's father, Friedrich Rosenthal."

"Papa, this is Krysia Smok."

She tilts her head. "Rosenthal, the writer?"

He shifts, uncomfortable with the attention. "I've written a few academic books, yes."

"I'm more acquainted with your articles." How is Krysia, a pianist from Poland, familiar with my father? "I particu-

larly enjoy your work on the interplay between the suffrag-
ist cause and socialism," she adds, animated now.

Papa bows slightly. "I'm humbled. And I'd be delighted
to discuss the subject with you further if you'd like to come
around for tea tomorrow. For now, I must excuse myself.
Margot, I'm afraid I need to stay to speak with one of the
British representatives after this." He pats my cheek. "The
car will be out front for you. Don't wait up for me. I shall
see you in the morning."

When he has gone, I turn back to Krysia. "How do you
know my father's work?"

"His writings on the advancement of women in the
communist system have been very helpful to the suffrag-
ist cause."

"Papa isn't a communist," I reply quickly, though I've
never read Papa's work myself.

She doesn't hear me, or pretends not to. "I detest pure
academics. But your father, well, he was quite active in the
protests in his day." Papa out of his study is an animal removed from natural habitat; it is difficult to fathom him
on the streets, chanting angrily like the Serb nationalists in
front of the foreign ministry on the Quai d'Orsay. There is
much about him, I realize, that I do not know.

Her gaze travels the room and stops on the catering manager who has entered the salon and is staring at us. The reception is winding down and Krysia is meant to be playing
as the guests leave, not talking. "It was a pleasure meeting
you," she says, shuffling through her sheet music.

"Come to tea tomorrow," I press. I'm lonely for company beyond the superficial chatter of the parties and I've

enjoyed these few brief moments of conversation more than any since our arrival.

She shakes her head, demurring. "Is it because we are German?"

"Of course not." Her tone is sincere. "I have a prior obligation. Another time."

"Here." I reach into my pocket and pull out one of the calling cards that Tante Celia had insisted I need. They seemed so frivolous at the time, but I'm glad to have them now. "In case you change your mind."

"Thank you." Krysia puts the card in her pocket in a way that tells me she will never use it.

She resumes playing and I walk from the salon, deflated. In the main ballroom, the gathering has begun to dissipate. I make my way to the cloakroom and when I return, the piano bench is empty.

Outside, I scan the line of cars and find ours. There is a dampness to the frosty night air that I can almost taste. As I get in, I see Krysia walking from the hotel with her parents. She kisses them each on the cheek and starts in the other direction, her blue cape radiant in the sea of black. I watch as she slips away, quiet as a cat, then ducks into the alleyway before reaching the boulevard.

Where is she going alone at night? It is after ten and there is still a curfew. I climb from the car once more. "I'll make my own way," I say to the driver, shutting the door before he can protest.

I weave my way through the departing crowd, breaking free and turning down the alleyway where I last saw Krysia. The street is dark and I fear that I have lost her, but I hear footsteps ahead and quicken my pace. A moment later the passageway opens onto a wide avenue and Krysia appears in a yellow pool of streetlight. She moves swiftly, almost seeming to fly beneath the billowing cape. I struggle to stay back far enough so as not to be noticed.

Krysia reaches the corner and stops. Then she turns, facing me before I have time to hide. "You again!" I freeze, an animal trapped. "Are you following me?"

"No—" I protest too quickly.

"I was joking, of course. You're staying in the area?"

"My hotel is nearby, but I am going to visit some friends." I regret the lie as soon as I have spoken, the notion that I would be calling on anyone at this hour of the night hardly plausible.

She does not respond but continues walking, shrugging her shoulders in a way that suggests I am welcome to join her. We travel wordlessly along the rue Royale, the swish of her cape giving off a faint hint of lilac perfume.

"Did you come to Paris before the war?" I ask, hoping she will not mind conversation. My breath rises in tiny puffs of frost.

"Yes. There was not so much work for pianists in southern Poland." She unfurls detail a bit at a time, like a kite string, or thread off a spool. "When the war broke out I found myself stranded here." There is something deeper beneath the surface, a longing in her voice that belies a part of the story she is not willing to share with me. "But I miss home terribly. Do you?"

"I suppose." I have not until just this moment thought about it. Our town house in Berlin's Jewish quarter is not large—even as a child, I could touch both walls of my bedroom at the same time if I stretched my arms out sideways. But it is cozy and made beautiful by all of my mother's decorations, the floral trim and slipcovers that Papa never would have thought to do himself and that he has left untouched since she died. There's a tiny garden with a fountain in the back, a park down the road for strolling. It's been years since we've actually lived there for any period of time, though. "We've been abroad for so long. Now home is wherever Papa and I land with a place to lay our heads and books to read."

She smiles. "The vagabond lifestyle." We reach the steps of the metro, a dark cavernous hole I've passed before but never entered. Krysia stops. "Your friends," she says suddenly. For a moment I am confused. She is referring to my alibi for being out walking, the fact that we've long since left the neighborhood I purported to be visiting. "You really were following me." It is not a question.

"I just…" I falter.

"What is it that you want from me?"

I try to come up with another excuse and then decide to be honest. "Company. I'm bored," I say, my voice dangerously close to a whine.

Krysia arches an eyebrow. "Bored, in Paris?"

My statement must sound ludicrous. "Not with the city, exactly. It's all of the parties and silly gossip."

"So don't go. Play your own game. No good can come from idleness. Come."

The metro steps are damp and slick and I take care not to fall as I follow her down. Below, my senses are assaulted by the dank odor of garbage and waste. I avert my eyes from a pair of rats scurrying along the tracks, fighting the urge to yelp. The ground rumbles beneath our feet and a long wooden train rolls into the station, looking not unlike the trolley cars that travel the streets above. The car we board is empty but for an old man sleeping at the other end. It begins to move swiftly through the darkness. I try to act normal, as though accustomed to this strange mode of travel.

"I saw you at the arrival parade for Wilson," I say, unable to hold back. Krysia stares vaguely over my shoulder and for a minute I doubt my memory, wondering if the woman at the parade had been someone else. "You left in the middle," I press. The statement comes out abrupt and intrusive.

"I had somewhere to be." She does not elaborate.

Two stops later the doors open and I follow Krysia back up onto the street, breathing in the fresh air deeply to clear the dankness from my lungs. We are on the Left Bank now, with its narrow, winding streets. This is Paris as I knew it as a girl, buildings leaning close, whispering secrets to one another. Parisians, still in the habit of conserving from the war, have shuttered and darkened their houses and only every other streetlight splutters in an attempt to save electricity. A low fog has rolled in from the river now, swirling eerily around us.

A few minutes later, we reach the boulevard du Montparnasse. The wide avenue is as bright as midday, light spilling forth from beneath the café awnings. A door to a café opens and a woman's high tinkling laugh cascades over the music. *La Closerie des Lilas* reads the painted sign on the glass window of the café, smaller print advertising the billiards and rooms available on the floors above.

I follow Krysia inside, where she weaves through a maze of tables without waiting to be seated, steering toward the high mahogany bar with red leather stools. Shelves filled with bottles climb to the ceiling of the mirrored wall behind it. The room is warm and close, plumed with clouds of cigarette smoke. Ragtime music from an unseen gramophone plays lively in the background, mixing with boisterous conversation in French, German and a handful of other languages.

Behind the bar, a skinny brown-haired boy, eighteen or nineteen maybe, with coal-black eyes, stacks beer steins. Feeling his gaze follow me, I flush. I'm still not used to the kind of attention young women receive in Paris, so much more admiring and less veiled than in London or Berlin.

We reach an alcove behind the bar, not quite set off enough from the main part of the café to be its own room, a few tables with an odd assortment of chairs thrown haphazardly around them. A half-decorated Christmas tree lists in the corner.

Krysia pulls up two chairs to one of the tables, where a handful of men are gathered. I await the introductions that do not come, then sit down beside her. The marble table is littered with overflowing ashtrays and empty wine bottles and an untouched carafe of still water. Two candles in a brass dish burn at the center, melting together in a molten pool. The only woman, Krysia looks out of place in this group of rough men. But she chats easily, as if among family. The gathering crackles with conversation. Across from me two men are debating how the war will be remembered in the literature, while to my left there is a lively discussion about the future of Palestine. Ideas rise like champagne bubbles around me and I struggle to keep up, to grasp one before it is displaced by the next

"Is Marcin coming?" one of the men asks in accented French. His sideburns, wide and deep, lash onto his cheeks like daggers. He wears a red silk scarf around his neck, knotted jauntily.

Krysia shakes her head. "He's playing a wedding at Chartres."

The man snorts. "That's a disgrace."

"One has to eat," Krysia replies vaguely, then turns to me. "Marcin is my husband."

"Oh." Krysia seems so solitary and stoic, an island unto herself. It is hard to imagine her needing or living with anyone.

"He plays cello."

An older man, fiftyish and portly with a shock of white hair, pads over to the table and places fresh, foaming mugs of beer in front of us. "She's too modest." His vowels are rounded, as though his cheeks were full, a Russian accent unmuted by his time in France. "Marcin is one of the foremost cellists in Europe," the man informs me. He begins twirling a coin between the knuckles of his left hand, index finger, middle, ring, pinky, and then back again without stopping. His fat fingers, each a sizable sausage, are surprisingly nimble. "He should be playing filled concert halls, not background music for wedding guests munching on canapés and cheap wine."

The red-scarfed man beside me raises his glass. "Hear, hear." His words are slurred.

Krysia pats the arm of the man who has handed us our drinks. "Margot, this principled fellow is Ignatz Stein." I am surprised to hear her introduce the barman as a friend. "He owns this place." I take a sip too large, caught off guard by the full, cold taste of hops, carrying me back to the fields of Bavaria in late harvest when Papa and I hiked there years earlier. The extra liquid spills out of the corner of my mouth. I reach for a napkin and, seeing none, furtively blot at the moisture with my sleeve, hoping no one will notice. Krysia turns to the man seated beside her. "And this is Deo Modigliani."

"The artist?" I cannot help but blurt out, awestruck. I have studied his work, seen it in the finest galleries and museums. Yet here he is sitting in this nondescript café and drinking beer like everyone else. I've heard of this Paris, artists and writers gathering in the Montparnasse cafés to drink and share ideas. It exists beneath the surface, separate and secret from the pomp and formality of the conference and everyday life overhead.

Krysia does not answer but turns her attention to a debate on the future of Alsace-Lorraine that has heated up at the far end of the table. "Surely the territory will be returned to France now." I have not been introduced to the man who is speaking.

"If the Americans and the French don't tear one another apart first," Krysia interjects. I nod. The conference is just days old and things had reportedly gotten quite contentious already.

"But the Americans…"

"It is quite easy to have views from halfway around the globe." Her observation is unfair and yet at the same time true. The Americans came to help with the fighting and they are here to help make the peace. Yet they will return home, largely unscathed by what is decided here. So why are they at the center of it?

She continues, "If the conference is to be democratic, then why is so much being done by the Big Four behind closed doors? And where is Russia?" I watch in awe as Krysia speaks her mind in a forthright way, mixing logic and passion in the way of a woman long accustomed to debate. Holding court, she appears ethereal, bathed in light. I have seldom heard women offer up opinions and have never seen them received with such respect. There is a keen intensity to the way she speaks, her voice low and melodic and commanding, that makes her somehow beautiful.

"Did you hear a kitchen boy from the Orient sent Wilson a petition for his country's freedom?" Modigliani offers, changing the subject.

"Ask Margot about it," Krysia says, gesturing toward me with her head. "I was playing in one of the salons, but she saw the whole thing."

"You were at the Wilson reception?" The barman, Ignatz, comes up to my chair, regarding me with newfound interest.

"Yes, my father is with the conference."

"Her father is Friedrich Rosenthal," Krysia adds with emphasis. Heads nod in recognition.

"Your father doesn't write under a nom de plume," Ignatz observes, still twirling a coin.

"No, why should he?"

"I think Ignatz only meant that not every writer has the courage to speak of such things in his own name," Krysia clarifies. *Courage.* I recall the news from back home in Berlin, the violence that had erupted as a result of the civil unrest. Politicians has been shot for no more than their views. Could Papa and the other academics be in similar danger?

Modigliani leans in, his artist eyes soulful. "And what are you, *ma petite?*"

"Deo," Krysia warns in a low voice, protective like an older sister.

I am uncertain how to answer. "I'm engaged," I offer. My response is met with blank stares around the table.

"I believe," Krysia prompts gently, "that he was asking what you are planning to do now that the war is over?" Krysia's clarification is of little help. Before the war, my future was clear—marriage to Stefan, the biggest question being whether to live with Papa indefinitely or save for an apartment of our own. That world is gone now. But still the old ties and expectations remain.

"I don't know," I confess finally. The room is warm and wobbly from the beer.

"How exciting." I search for sarcasm in her voice and find none. "Starting fresh, reborn out of the ashes. The war was horrible, but it has shaken things up, given each of us a chance to stake a claim for what she wants."

"They say that Kolchak's Whites are making gains at Perm…" Ignatz offers, turning the topic to Russia. I sit back, grateful to no longer be the focus. But I find the topic unsettling. Russia has become a wild land since the czar was taken down, his whole family murdered. The Bolsheviks are in charge, or at least most think so—the country has largely been cut off from the West and so only rumors trickle out.

"Papa says we need to engage with the Whites as well as the Bolsheviks," I say, speaking up in spite of my own desire to remain inconspicuous. I fight to keep the uncertainty from my voice. But I sound childish, falling back on my father's opinions as if I have none of my own. "That is, perhaps we can help them to form some sort of coalition government...." I falter, unaccustomed to the eyes on me. Even the dark-eyed boy behind the bar appears to be listening with interest. I have discussed politics with Papa all my life, but never in a public forum such as this.

"What else does Papa say?" Ignatz asks from where he stands behind Krysia, a note of chiding to his voice.

"That the conference will move quickly to act before Russia can subsume too much territory." I speak quickly now, too far gone to stop. "With a quick vote on recognition of the new Croat-Serb state, for example. The vote is to take place as soon as the conference opens. And it seems that Wilson and Lloyd George are favorably predisposed to a Pan-Slavic nation. But Clemenceau is likely to side with Orlando and the Italians and hold it up...."

"They can vote all they want. Lenin will not compromise on any sort of coalition," Krysia remarks. She is talking about the Bolshevik leader not with the same fear I've heard at the parties, but with a kind of hushed reverence.

"You're communist?" I ask, recalling her description of Papa's work.

"I detest labels," she replies coolly. "I'd say socialist, really, though there's nothing wrong with communism as an ideal."

Thinking of the stories I've read about Russia, I shudder. "It's anarchy. They destroy businesses and overthrow leaders. They murdered the czar's whole family, even the children."

"That's the problem with Germans," one of the men scoffs derisively. "No stomach for reform. As Lenin says, revolution will never come to Berlin because the Germans would want to queue up for it."

"It's a shame that social change has to be accomplished by such violent means," Krysia says before I can respond to the insult. "Though the previous rulers were hardly saints. Really the ideas behind communism of equal contributions and distributions are good. But they're being corrupted for power just like any other ideology."

One of the men snorts. "Bah! The socialists are too weak to act on their principles. We can sit around here talking all night and it will do nothing. We need to do something."

"Raoul…" Krysia says, and there is an undercurrent of warning to her voice. "We should go," she adds abruptly.

I've offended her, I fret. But the gathering has begun to break up, and around us everyone is gathering their coats and reaching for their pockets for a few loose francs. I picture guiltily Papa's allowance money folded neatly in my purse. Should I offer to pay? Only Modigliani sits motionless. "Am I to accept another drawing from you?" Ignatz asks him chidingly. I notice then that the wall behind the bar is covered with artwork, framed paintings and hastily pinned sketches to pay for food and drink. The artist does not answer, but stares into the distance, his eyes heavy lidded.

"You'll see him home?" Krysia asks Ignatz, then turns to me without waiting for a response. "Spirits help the creative soul to a point," she says in a low voice, as we make our way through the main room of the café. The crowd has ceded to the curfew, leaving beer bottles and overflowing ashtrays in their wake. "And then they destroy it."

"Monsieur Modigliani, will he be all right?"

She nods. "Stein will kick him out at some point. Otherwise a good number of them would stay all night—these days, it's cheaper than heating their flats."

"So many artists. I'd heard of such things, but I had no idea…."

"They suffered during the war like everyone else with lack of food and money. But now they're trying to recapture the lost time, the frenzy of life. And art is such a solitary business. Coming together like this gives them a sense of companionship. Though with all of the drinking and such, it's a marvel they get any work done at all."

Outside the night is icy. "What did that man, Raoul, I believe you called him, mean about 'doing something'?"

She hesitates. "Nothing. They all like to talk big when they drink. What could a few artists do, anyway? It's just that the way the peace conference is being conducted, it will still only be justice for some, a gift from the powerful if they choose to be beneficent. But true freedom is innate—given not by man but from God herself." My jaw drops slightly at Krysia's reference to God as a female.

Krysia hails a taxi and holds the door for me. I slide across the seat to make room for her. She does not get in, but starts to hand the driver some bills. "My flat is nearby," she explains.

"I have money," I say.

"Well, get home safely. And Deo is right. You should figure out what you want to do."

"Do?"

"With your life. Self-determination isn't just some abstract political notion, intended for the masses. Each of us must decide whom she will be, what we want for ourselves." I had not thought about it in such a manner. "You're not bored," she observes. "You're restless. Bored suggests a lack of interest in the world around you. But you drink in everything and can't get enough. The world has come to Paris and you're at the center of it all," she adds. "The question now is what you do with it."

I see myself then as undefined, a lump of clay. "But I'm just an observer." In that moment, I grasp my own frustration—I am tired of just watching things play out in front of me like a performance on a stage. I want to take part.

"Why?" she demanded. "Why not allow yourself even for a minute to step outside the box into which you were born?"

"My father. And there are other reasons. My fiancé was wounded...." I falter, swept by the urge to tell Krysia how I feel about Stefan.

"We all have pasts." Her tongue seems loosened by the

alcohol and I think she might say something about her mysterious errand to the park. "There's a new world being born," she observes. "We each might as well make what we want of it."

I look up at the dark slate of gray sky above, picturing the kitchen boy from the Orient, the one who was fighting for his country's independence among the dirty dishes and food scraps. If he was not daunted in his quest, then how could I be? I hadn't until this very moment seen the opportunity in all of the change, rules and norms discarded.

"Make Paris your own," she exhorts again. "Do something, write something, take a class. You are young and unattached, at least for the moment." I hold my breath, waiting for her to ask about my fiancé, but she continues. "You're in one of the world's greatest cities at the dawn of the modern age. You have resources, wits, talent. There's no greater sin than to waste all of that. Find your destiny." Before I can ask her how, she turns and disappears into the night.

3

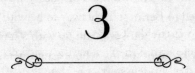

I sit in the stillness of the study, the room dim but for the pale light that filters in, silhouetting the windowpane. Beyond the lattice of dark wood, the robin's-egg-blue sky is laced with soft white clouds. A rolling wave of slate-gray domes and spires spills endlessly across the horizon, poking out from the haze that shrouds the city like a wreath. Bells chime unseen in the distance.

I wrap my hands around the too-hot cup of tea that sits before me on the table, then release it again and gaze down at the front page of yesterday's *Le Journal*. The early mornings have always been mine. Papa loves to work long into the night, a lone lamp at the desk pooling yellow on the papers below. As a child, I often fell asleep to the sweet smell of pipe smoke, the sound of his pen scratching on the paper a familiar lullaby.

I eye the letter I'd started writing to Stefan the previous evening. I had written to him regularly when we were in England, of course. But I have not put pen to paper since our arrival in Paris simply because I did not know what to say about the fact that I had come here instead of going home.

I reread my words. *I attended the welcome reception for Wilson and it was quite the affair…* I crumple the piece of paper and throw it in the wastebasket. I feel foolish talking of parties and Paris while he lies wounded in a hospital bed. Why had I not returned to Berlin straightaway to be with him? Stefan is so loyal. Once, when I was laid up with a sprained ankle, he faithfully brought me my school assignments each afternoon and carried my completed work back to school each morning for a week. He would not have left me alone if the situation was reversed. I am not abandoning him, though. I will go back as soon as the conference is over.

Starting on a fresh sheet of crisp stationery, I decide to be more forthright: *I'm sorry not to be there with you. Papa was summoned to the conference and I did not want him to travel alone.* Then I pause. Stefan has never begrudged me my relationship with my father, the way that Papa seemed to come first and would always be central in our lives. But he would know that Papa had Celia here to look after him. I try again: *Papa had to come directly to Paris and did not want me to travel back to Germany alone.* Though the explanation is still unsatisfactory, I set down my pen.

I stand and pick up Papa's hat from the chair. Wrapped up in his thoughts, he's prone to dropping things and leaving them where they fall. I run my hand along the felt brim, too wide to be fashionable now. *With love, Lucy,* reads the now-faded embroidery along the inside band. It was a gift from my mother, worn beyond repair.

Reflexively, I continue straightening the room, moving books to piles in the corners, sweeping a few missed crumbs from the table. We've managed to accumulate a sizable bit of clutter, even in the short time we've been here. There are a handful of cozy touches—a small vase of gardenias on the windowsill, a throw across the settee—all courtesy of Tante Celia, who is domestic in a way that I could never be.

In the corner are the discarded boxes that had contained Uncle Walter's Hanukah presents. The holidays had passed quietly, Papa so immersed in work before the formal opening of the conference he had scarcely paused. Too much celebrating would have been unseemly, anyway, with all of the suffering, the homeless and wounded that linger at every corner. But Uncle Walter, unaware of the subtle context here, had sent boxes of gifts: slippers and a wrap for me, new ties and shirtwaists for Papa. He'd sent money, too, more than we had seen in some time, with special instructions that I was to have my wedding gown made. Included was a remnant of lace and a picture of my mother's dress for the tailor to copy.

Picking up the lace now, my throat tightens. The gift contains a silent message—that I am to do what is expected of me, play along as I always have. This time in Paris is not a license to step out of line, but merely a brief sojourn before I marry Stefan.

Stefan had proposed the Sunday after the war broke out on a walk by the lake behind the villa. "If you'll marry me when I get back…"

I hesitated. Stefan and I had been formally courting for just over a year, the transition from friendship to romance marked rather unceremoniously by a brief conversation between him and Papa. Yet despite the exclusivity of our relationship and the time that had passed, I hadn't given thought to the future. But the war had sped up the film, bringing the question to the glaring light of day. "Why rush things?"

His eyes widened with disbelief. "I'm going to war, Margot." For the first time then I saw real fear, portending all that was to come.

"I know. But they say it will be quick—weeks, maybe a month or two at worst case. Then you'll be back and we'll decide things properly." He did not answer but continued staring at me, pleading. I swallowed. Marriage felt so adult and constraining, so permanent. Stefan asked little of me, but he was asking for this now.

I thought of the dance Stefan and I had attended months earlier. At first it had been an awkward affair—most students had not come as couples and boys and girls lingered separately back against the walls, barely speaking. Then a few people shuffled to the middle of the dance floor and gradually others joined them. I had gazed at Stefan hopefully and, seemingly encouraged, he extended his hand. But before he could speak, Helmut, a thick-necked boy, walked over. "Would you like to dance?" he asked me, so forcefully it was hardly a question. I looked up at Stefan helplessly—I had come with him and I wanted to dance with him, at least for the first song. But he shrugged, unwilling to struggle. If Stefan could not stand up for himself at a dance, how would he ever survive war? He needed the promise of our marriage to keep him strong.

The war was coming, I told myself; we would all need to make sacrifices. "Well, then," I said. Marriage was to be my own personal conscription. "Yes, I would love to be your wife."

We walked back to the house to share the good news. "You don't mind, do you, that he didn't have time to ask permission?" I asked Papa. "I mean, with the war and all."

"He had asked my permission some time ago," Papa confided. So Stefan had this planned all along. The war had just been an excuse to move things up.

The quiet clicking of the door leading from Papa's room into the hallway stirs me from my thoughts. Tante Celia keeps her own apartment in a town house in the 16th arrondissement that I've not visited, a fiction designed for public appearances as well as for my benefit. Once, when I was not more than twelve, I spied her leaving our house in Berlin before dawn, head low beneath the hood of her cloak. At the time I was incensed: How dare they soil the memory of my mother—how dare he? Older now, I do not begrudge Papa company and warmth. He seems so much happier with her nearby than he had been in England, where Celia could not get a visa to join us. She is just so plain and uninteresting, a shadow of her beautiful older sister. Though perhaps that is why Papa likes her—she is the closest reminder of my mother.

My gaze travels to the photograph of the tall, willowy woman on the mantelpiece, taken in our Berlin garden before I was born. My mother had been an actress before marrying my father, leaving home at the age of sixteen and performing around the world to great acclaim against her family's wishes. Papa had seen her in a performance of *As You Like It* in Amsterdam and had been so taken with her portrayal of Rosalind that he had sent flowers backstage with an invitation to dinner. Six months later they wed and she left the stage for good.

I study the photo, which Papa brings with him wherever we go and puts out as soon as we arrive. Her pose, one hand on hip, the other outstretched slightly with palm upward, is beguiling, yet somehow natural. Mother and I shared the same pale skin and almond-shaped eyes, but her dark hair was smooth, not kinked and unruly like mine. Ten years have passed, and my actual memories of our time together are dim. To me, she is a shadowy figure with a sad expression and hollow eyes, a woman who never seemed to sit still or truly be present.

I return to my chair and wrap my hands around the warm cup of tea, watching as a flock of starlings rises from one of the cathedral spires, startled by a noise I did not hear. My thoughts turn to Krysia. It has been weeks since she put me in the taxi. I had hoped she might call or send word inviting me out to join her circle of friends again. The longing for company is strange to me. I've never had female friends. Even in school, I tended to play with the boys, enjoying the pure physicality of sport where it was permitted. But the excitement of the evening I spent at the bar with Krysia has left me hoping to see her again.

She has not contacted me, though. Did I embarrass her with my lack of substance? A few nights earlier there was a gala and I attended more eagerly than usual, urging Papa to dress promptly. But a string orchestra played waltzes, the piano in the corner deserted and silent.

Restless, I finish my tea and dress, then scribble a note for Papa before putting on my coat and gloves and leaving the apartment. On the street, I pause. It is January now, the pavement altogether too icy for biking, so I begin to walk, making my way toward the river. As I near the wide expanse of water, the wind, no longer buttressed by the buildings, blows sharply. Drawing my coat tight, I cross the arched pont de la Concorde. On the far bank sits the wide expanse of the Quai d'Orsay. Though it is not yet seven o'clock, the crowds of demonstrators, protesting for their causes and seeking to be heard, have already begun to form outside the tall iron gates of the foreign ministry where Wilson and the other powers labor to re-create the world.

I press forward, head low against the wind. Past the ministry and away from the water now, the streets begin to narrow. At the corner I pause, peering uneasily down a side street. Rue de Courty is one that I have avoided for months. The center of the block is taken up by a wide building with columns that suggest it was once a government administration building of some sort. I passed it once shortly after our arrival in Paris, taken aback by the improbably young men in wheelchairs, who sat forlornly by the windows looking as though they are just acting parts in a play and in fact might jump up and walk at any second. Would they ever leave the hospital? What if there were no families to claim them? I had run from the block, haunted.

Now my guilt rises anew: Should I have gone back to Berlin and taken Stefan from the hospital, cared for him myself? The hospitals themselves could be as dangerous as war—nursing care was short and supplies minimal even in the best hospitals. Influenza and tuberculosis were rampant. If I went back to Germany now, perhaps I could get him out.

Unable to bear the cold any longer, I walk to the corner and hail a taxi. "Montparnasse," I say to the driver and it is only then that I fully realize I am going to try to find Krysia. "Rue Vavin," I add, recalling one of the major intersections. A few minutes later, I pay the driver and step out onto the pavement. The boulevard du Montparnasse is quiet at this early hour, the bars and cafés that seem to never sleep now briefly at rest. At La Closerie des Lilas, I peer through the glass into the darkened café. I push against the door expecting it to be locked, but it opens.

"Bonjour."

"Oui?" I step inside, adjusting my eyes to the dim lighting. Ignatz is behind the counter, alone in the otherwise deserted room. Last time I was here the café felt almost magical, but in the crude light of day it is a dirty room, trash from the previous evening still littering the floor, ordinary in a way that makes me wonder if I imagined the revelry of the earlier night. "Ah, the ambassador's daughter." His tone is mocking.

I consider pointing out that the title more aptly describes Krysia than me, then decide against it. "Margot Rosenthal," I correct.

"Mademoiselle Rosenthal." He gives a mock bow, then throws a handful of spoons into one of the bins with a clatter. "Of course. How can I help you?" His voice is gravelly.

"Krysia…that is, I haven't heard from her in a few weeks and I was worried."

"I haven't seen her. She's sick. The grippe, or some such thing."

So that is why she hasn't contacted me. I'm relieved and concerned at the same time. "Is it serious?"

He shrugs. "I shouldn't think so, or I would have heard. She's got Marcin to look after her."

His answer does little to assuage my fear. "I'd like to check on her if you'd be so kind as to provide her address."

I hold my breath, expecting him to object, but he pulls out a scrap of paper and scribbles on it. "It's not far from here. If you walk up rue d'Assas, you'll find it just before you reach boulevard Saint-Germain." He starts to slide the paper across the bar, then stops, leaving my hand dangling expectantly in midair. "I'm glad you're here, actually."

"Oh?"

Ignatz steps out from behind the bar. "*Oui.* You had so many interesting things to say the other night." He is larger than I remembered from last time I was here, reminding me of a grizzly bear.

Warmth creeps up my back. I never should have spoken about Papa's work. I replay that night in the bar in my head, my tongue loosened by beer, too eager to say something meaningful and curry favor with the group. "It was nothing."

"No, you had real views."

I flush. "I never should have spoken at all."

"Nonsense. Your wit added much to the discussion. But it also caused me to think, your contribution can be of most use to our cause."

"I'm afraid I don't quite understand."

"As you may have gathered the other night, we're interested in politics quite a bit. We're more than just a ragtag group of artists and innkeepers. Some of us—not all but some—are actually doing something to further our beliefs in a just world." What could they do, I want to ask. Write about freedom? Lobby for it? "You do believe that people should have the right to self-determination, don't you?"

"Yes." But I remember then my conversation with Papa about the limits of what could be done at the conference, the fact that not everyone's claim to autonomy could be granted.

"We gather information, pass it on to Moscow or others who might be in a position to further those aims. You can help us if you'd like."

I hesitate. What could I possibly do? He continues. "The information you shared about the Serbia vote was most helpful. If your father should say anything else…"

I cut him off. "He seldom speaks about his work."

"Your father would not mind—ours and his cause are one and the same. I daresay he would want to help us himself, but for his position."

Krysia had been so excited about Papa's work. Maybe their interests really are aligned. "Perhaps…"

"So if you hear something of interest about what the Big Four might do…"

"I'll tell Krysia," I finish, regretting the words almost before they are out of my mouth.

"Oh, I wouldn't burden her," he interjects hurriedly. "She's so caught up in her music. Best to let me know personally."

Not answering, I snatch the paper with Krysia's address

and make my way out to the street, half-expecting him to try to stop me from leaving. The fractured cobblestones point in different directions, beckoning me to follow. Did Ignatz seriously think that I could—or would—help him?

Soon, I stop before the address Ignatz had given me. I step forward, studying the narrow four-story building. There is an iron gate overgrown with ivy, a small courtyard behind it leading to an arched wood door with carvings and a brass knocker at its center. The note indicates that Krysia lives on the top floor, but when I peer upward the shutters are drawn tight. Musicians, like artists, I suppose, work long into the night, and shut out the indecency of early morning. It is not yet ten o'clock, my arrival unannounced. I turn away, suddenly aware of the impulsiveness of my coming here. I should have asked Ignatz if Krysia had a telephone or perhaps had him forward a message. But I continue to stare upward, wishing I could somehow reach her.

"Hello," a familiar voice says behind me. I turn to face Krysia in her blue cape. Contrary to what Ignatz had said, she does not look ill.

I notice then the rosary beads clutched in her right hand. "You were at church?"

She nods. "The old parish church at Saint-Séverin."

"You're devout," I marvel. How does her faith mesh with her communist political views?

She ignores my remark. "Come in." If she is put off by my unexpected visit, she gives no indication, but opens the door then steps aside to let me in. The lobby is dim and in disrepair but the banister carvings are ornate, belying a once-fine home. Paned windows swung inward to let in the fresh air, which carries a hint of smoke.

I follow her up the winding staircase, hanging back as she unlocks the door. She does not speak but walks to a tiny kitchen in the corner and puts on the kettle. The flat is just a single room, tall narrow windows overlooking a stone courtyard. The space is cozy, large pillows, everything in a maroon and gold reminiscent of something from India. There are books stacked in the corners, rich paintings on the wall. There is no table and I wonder where they eat. A candle, now extinguished, gives off a cinnamon smell.

I stand in the entranceway, clutching my gloves. To have shown up unannounced is bad enough, but I do not intend to overstay. A moment later, she carries two cups of coffee to the cushioned seat by the window. "Please, come sit."

I take off my coat. "Your flat is lovely," I remark, as I perch on the edge of the settee.

She waves her hand. "It's a fine little place. We've been here since before the war, when the neighborhood was less in fashion."

What might my own apartment be like? A vision pops into my mind of a garret like this, with lots of windows and light, a nook where I could drink my breakfast tea and gaze out the window. I'm not sure of the city in which my fantasy apartment exists—back in Berlin just steps from Papa, or somewhere farther away?

A cat slips quietly around the base of the chair before jumping up and folding itself into Krysia's lap. I'm surprised—I've seen almost no pets since we've been back in Paris, none of the poodles and little terriers on leashes that littered the parks before the war. There are the strays, of course, animals too large and mangy to have been anyone's pet for long, hurrying busily between the rubbish piles in the side streets. But there wasn't enough food for the people during the war, much less animals, and it was a mercy I'm sure to put one's beloved pet to sleep rather than let it starve. Some were probably eaten.

Through the floorboards comes a lively, unrecognizable tune from a gramophone. "I'm so sorry to intrude," I apologize again.

"Not at all. Artists are a bit reclusive, but back home in Poland there are none of these formalities. Guests are always welcome at a moment's notice."

Relaxing somewhat, I take the cup she offers. "I hadn't seen you. And then I heard that you were sick."

She waves her hand dismissively. "Just a bad cold. These things get so exaggerated." But there are circles beneath her eyes that suggest something more. She takes a sip of coffee, savoring it with relish. Coffee, like so many things, was scarce during the war, the ersatz mix of ground nuts and grains hardly a substitute.

My body goes slack with relief. "I was worried." The fullness of my voice reveals my concern.

"It's good to know that someone might notice if I dropped off the face of the earth." She smiles faintly, her tone wry.

The cat hops across into my lap, purring low and warm. "She doesn't like most people," Krysia observes approvingly.

We drink our coffee in silence. Something about her absence and her tired expression do not make sense. I take a deep breath, then dive in. "Krysia, I wanted to ask you about the young women in the park."

She blinks. "How do you know about that?"

"When you left Wilson's reception, you went to the park...."

"You followed me then, too?" she asks, cutting me off.

"No. That is...I was curious where you were going and why." I falter. "I guess I did follow you."

"And I should ask the question—why exactly?" She has a point. We've spoken twice, spent a few hours together—hardly the kind of intimate friendship that warrants such probing questions.

"I was concerned."

"You were curious," she corrects. I was both, I concede inwardly. Of course I wanted to know what she was doing, understand her mystery. But I feel a certain kinship to Krysia, more so than I should for a woman I've only just met.

"Years ago I had a child," she says, her voice a monotone. I stifle my shock. Whatever I had expected Krysia to say, it wasn't that. "I was twenty-two when I got pregnant." Just about the age I am now, though I cannot fathom the experience. "Old enough to make my own choices. The father—it wasn't Marcin back then—was long since gone." I struggle not to reach for her. "My parents wanted me to have it taken care of, to avoid the scandal that would have devastated them socially. I made the appointment and even went. I couldn't go through with it, though. I had the baby." Her voice cracks slightly. "But I was too afraid to try to raise her on my own. So I gave her up."

Her. I remember the young women skating. One had

been taller than the rest, with chestnut hair not unlike Krysia's. She continues, "I go to the park each week to see her. Just once a week. Any more would only raise suspicion."

"Have you ever spoken to her?"

She shakes her head. "I have no wish to intrude and complicate her life. I've tried to do the right thing—letting her go when I couldn't support her, keeping an eye out for her safety. Yet it all gets twisted somehow. I mean, I had to give her up. But I can't just abandon her, can I, and go on as though she doesn't exist and this piece of me isn't out there in the world?" She sounds lost, no longer confident and strong but a child herself somehow. Krysia is caught in a kind of purgatory, unable to leave the child but unable to be with her.

"She's no longer a child. Perhaps if you spoke to her now, you could explain."

"There are some doors that are not meant to be opened." Her tone is firm.

I recall the girl, so similar to Krysia, except that she was slight, a thin slip of birch beside Krysia's oak. "She looks well cared for."

"The people who adopted her are good folks," she agrees. "A bit more materialistic and less cultured than I would have wanted. But there's time for that later, perhaps a year abroad, study at the Sorbonne." She sounds as though she is planning a future that she will somehow be a part of, though that, of course, is impossible.

"Perhaps," I soothe. I have no idea if she is right, but it is what she needs to hear. "Perhaps you'll have children of your own. More children," I add as she opens her mouth to protest that the girl is her own.

"Having Emilie nearly killed me." *Emilie.* I do not know if that is the child's actual name by her adopted parents, or just one Krysia uses in her mind. "She's seventeen. But she hasn't settled on a suitor that I can tell, I think because she is still studying." There is a note of pride in Krysia's voice, as if through her estranged child she could correct the mistakes of her own youth.

"I've never told anyone." Underlying her voice is a plea that I not judge her choices. "I don't know why I'm telling you." *Because I caught you,* I want to say. But she could have lied to me, made up a story about the girls in the park. No, there is something about me that she trusts almost instinctively. I've always had that way about me, that makes people want to talk and share.

"What about your parents?"

"There was a time they would not speak to me. Now we're civil since we've put all that behind us." She places heavy irony on the last two words, as though acknowledging that it is anything but in the past.

"This week she didn't appear at the park. Listening to the others, I learned that she'd been taken ill." I understand then Krysia's absence, the circles beneath her eyes that came not from her own sickness but worry about her child. "It was the worst thing in the world. I wanted to go to her in the hospital but, of course, I couldn't. So I've been in church, praying almost nonstop for her recovery." No, madly liberal, communist Krysia was not religious. It was the helplessness and despair of a sick child she could not be with that had literally brought Krysia to her knees. "She's turned the corner now and is recovering."

Yet Krysia still prayed. "When I didn't see you for a time, I thought maybe I had said or done something to offend you," I say, changing the subject. Then I stop, realizing how insecure I sound.

"Not at all. I'm glad to know you. I have Marcin, of course, but I've forgotten how pleasant the company of another woman can be."

I nod. "Me, too." I am not comfortable in the company of women. I dislike their gossipy talk and the way they eye one another as if in constant competition. But Krysia is different somehow. For a minute I consider sharing Ignatz's request that I help provide information. But Ignatz bade me not tell her about our conversation, almost as if he considers her too vulnerable and weak to be trusted. I do not want to bother her now, while she is so worried about Emilie.

She picks up some knitting needles and yarn beside her. Her hands are so often in motion, playing the piano, knitting—like two birds she needs to keep occupied so they don't fly away.

"So have you made any decisions?" she asks abruptly.

"Excuse me?"

"When we last spoke, you were trying to figure out what you were going to do." She watches me expectantly, as though I was supposed to have remolded my life plan in a few short weeks. Why must I *do* at all? As a girl, no one expected me to do or be—I just *was,* a happy state of affairs that I should have liked to carry on indefinitely. In truth, our conversation and Krysia's challenge had prickled at me nonstop since our last meeting. But I have no new answers. There have always been expectations: I will be wife to Stefan, a mother someday if his condition still permits it. Those things just meant being an appendage to the lives of others, I see now. Could that possibly be enough?

"You have a real gift with words," she adds when I do not answer. "Have you ever considered being a writer?"

I laugh, toss my head. "A writer? What would I say? You have to have more than just words—you need life experience and I have so little of that."

"Where will you go after the conference?" she asks, trying an easier question.

"Back to Berlin with Papa, I suppose."

She scrutinizes her knitting, then pulls out a stitch. "Why? Why not see a bit of the world now, while you can?"

"But my fiancé…"

"Ah yes, you mentioned him the other night, fleetingly. Once you go back to him, there will be a wedding, then children. There will always be something to stop you. You only have right now. Go while you can."

"I'll go back to Stefan after the conference," I say stubbornly.

"You sound enthralled."

"I didn't mean it that way." But it isn't my tone that she has taken issue with—it is the fact that I am going back at all.

"Is that what you want?"

I start to say yes, then stop. It is a lie.

"Then why go?"

"Because he is my fiancé. And he was badly wounded."

I expect her to ask how he was hurt, the seriousness of his injuries. "Do you love him?" I'm not sure what love is, really. When I was fifteen, Stefan and our tiny neighborhood, the park where we would walk together, and our quiet cinema dates, were the only world I had ever known. Stefan would have changed during the war.

"I care for him."

"That isn't the same."

"I know." I turn to gaze out the window at the courtyard below. "I feel so differently now."

"Or maybe you feel the same, but you've changed and so those feelings are no longer enough."

I consider this. Part of me has always sensed that there were differences. I recall a conversation Stefan and I had once about my mother. I'd found an old playbill from a show she'd done in Morocco and shown it to him. "How exciting," I remarked, "to have traveled the world."

But Stefan had looked at me blankly. With everything he wanted right here in Berlin—his family and me—he had no desire to leave. "It must have been terribly difficult," he replied, "not to mention dangerous."

I could see it in his eyes, too, the day he left for the army. "You'll get to go so many places," I'd offered as we stood on the platform and said goodbye, trying to force optimism into my voice. "Belgium, Holland, maybe even France." But Stefan had never wanted to leave in the first place, whereas I could not wait to go. No, the differences were there even before the war, but it had taken the years apart to make me perceive them clearly. Now they are magnified, not just by time, but the ways in which I had changed, as well.

"Maybe," I reply to Krysia. "We were so young and four years apart feels like a lifetime. Sometimes he seems more like an idea than a person. I hate feeling this way. And he needs me."

"A sense of obligation is no way to start a life," she presses.

"Loyalty is important." My voice sounds tinny and weak.

"So is happiness. Would you want someone to marry you for such a reason?"

"No, of course not." But I am not lying wounded in a hospital bed, with no prospect of a future. I am suddenly annoyed. I barely know Krysia. Why is she asking me such things? "I should go." I stand and put on my coat. "Thank you for the coffee."

I half wish she will try to stop me, but she nods, rising. "Thank you for calling. I hope to see you again soon."

Outside it is warmer now, the late-morning sun taking away some of the chill. The sidewalks are now lively with pedestrians, merchants and deliverymen unloading crates from lorries. As I make my way toward the metro, Krysia's questions about Stefan prickle at me. I hear her voice, exhorting me to see the world now, while I still can. A thousand objections roar through my brain: I can't leave Papa. I can't travel alone.

Nothing has changed—my problems loom as large as ever. But despite my earlier annoyance, it felt good to share my fears about Stefan and a life together with Krysia, to verbalize to somebody the thoughts and feelings I'd barely dared to acknowledge to myself for so long. And Krysia confiding her story of Emilie helped, as well. Learning that someone as strong and self-assured as Krysia also wrestles with the past and the right thing to do makes me feel somehow less alone. She seems to enjoy my company, though perhaps I am simply a proxy for the daughter she so desperately wants to know but cannot. Squaring my shoulders, I start down the street with a lighter gait than I've had since before the war.

Forty minutes later, I reach our suite at the hotel. I open the door and stop. The curtains are drawn and only faint daylight filters in. A rustling noise at the desk startles me and I jump. Papa is here, hunched over the desk in the darkness, when he should have been at the ministry. "Papa?" Alarmed, I rush forward. He does not move. I put my hand on his shoulder, fearful that it is his heart and the worst has happened. "Papa, are you well?"

He straightens but his expression is dazed as though he does not see or recognize me. Before him on the desk sits a newspaper. "There's been an attempt on Clemenceau's life." I pick up the paper. My breath catches as I take in the photograph of the would-be assassin. The dark-eyed boy from the La Closerie des Lilas stares back at me.

"The attacker possessed information from the conference that was not public, information that prompted him to act." Papa drops his head to his hands once more. "And I'm afraid they're going to blame it on me."

PART TWO

Versailles, April 1919

4

I peer out the window down the road at the Hôtel des
Réservoirs. The six-story building, with its aged yellow
facade and arched doorway, stands behind hastily erected
barbed wire, giving it the feel of a fortress or prison, de-
pending upon whether one is to be kept in or out. Either
way, it looks as if the German delegation is to be quaran-
tined, defeat a virus that no one wants to catch. Apple blossoms frame the hotel in a defiant lush pink.

The road leading to the guarded hotel gate is lined three
deep with onlookers, reporters and photographers and
townspeople and those who had packed the trains down
from the city. There is no official party as there had been
when Wilson arrived, no military band or other pageantry
to herald the Germans' arrival—just hordes of the genu-
inely curious, waiting to see those who are to be held responsible for the world's suffering.

I turn back into the room where Papa sits working at his
desk, oblivious to the spectacle taking place across the road.
Our apartment in Versailles is located not in a hotel, but a
tall row house that has been converted into apartments to
accommodate the sudden influx. It is laid out much like
our previous quarters in the city, two bedrooms adjoined

by a common space. Everything, from Papa's piles of books to the photograph of my mother on the mantelpiece, is in the same location as in Paris. It is as if we travel in a shell, I'd decided when we first settled in, re-creating the identical living environment for ourselves in each city. But the rooms here are smaller and oddly shaped, the parlor something of a trapezoid, walls with faded flowered paper slanting inward from the windows.

"They should be here soon," I say. Papa does not answer. He had not wanted to be here today—or at all for that matter. He had tried to lure me away with an excursion to Paris. But I had insisted that we stay, despite his derisiveness of what he called the "circus of shame." He does not stand at the window himself, but busies himself at the desk. How can he not look?

The topic had come up at a dinner party three weeks earlier when it was announced that the Germans had finally been summoned to the conference. "You'll move over to Versailles now, of course, and stay with the delegation?" someone asked Papa. Until that point we had enjoyed our neutral status, not being identified too closely with any one camp, including the defeated. But when a telegram came from the head of the delegation inviting us to relocate, Papa could avoid it no longer. So we left the city for this dreary little suburb of Versailles, though he still commutes almost daily to the conference proceedings at the ministry in Paris.

Our apartment is just across the road and down a bit from the hotel. The location, close by the German residence but not within, reflects the delicate role Papa must play. The conference does not trust him because he is German. The

German delegation will surely not accept Papa because he has been part of the conference. We are an island.

"I'm going to market," I say, unable to stand the confinement of the apartment any longer and eager to get a closer view. Unlike the hotel in Paris, there's no kitchen to deliver our meals and the town's few remaining restaurants are dismal affairs, so it falls to me to procure what we need.

I hold my breath, waiting for Papa to see through my excuse—the shops are likely to be closed now with the arrival. But he does not. Papa has been more preoccupied than ever these past few months since the attempt on Clemenceau's life. Though the French prime minister recovered quickly and the story faded from the newspapers, it continued to hang over Papa and me, a silent dagger.

I almost told Papa that night that it was my fault. "Quite a shock," he'd remarked. "Clemenceau will be fine, even joked as they were taking him to the hospital about the madman's poor marksmanship. But it is a sobering reminder to us all that even while we are here working toward the new world, there are those who would derail it." His brow furrowed.

"What is it? Is there something more?"

"Not at all."

"You don't need to shield me. I'm not a child."

He smiled. "No, of course not. I never like to trouble you and give pause to your beautiful smile, even for a moment. It's just that this may cause trouble for me. Cottin—the would-be assassin—was upset about French opposition to the Pan-Slavic state. We had been trying to keep it a secret so the media controversy would not keep us from getting the matter done. The assassination attempt, the timing of it, gives rise to suspicions that someone had leaked information about the vote."

"But surely no one could think that you had a role."

Papa, the only German detailed to the conference, not to mention a Jew, feared himself a likely scapegoat. I watched his face, wondering if he suspected me, or was perhaps even hinting. But he could not imagine that I would have betrayed him in such a fashion. "I appreciate your outrage on my behalf. It will be fine."

Though the accusations had never become overt, there had been a quiet distancing between Papa and some of the other conference advisors that made our sojourn to Versailles almost a relief.

Studying Papa now, my guilt rises anew. Only I know the truth—that it was my careless remark, overheard at the bar, which gave Cottin the information to act. I have never been good at keeping secrets from Papa and I have struggled for months not to blurt out what I had done, to seek his forgiveness. But he has enough to deal with right now and I won't strain his health further.

Down on the street, the morning air is warming and a bit stale with gutter stench. Across the road the hulking Versailles palace sits with its endless fountains and gardens, swallowing the tiny town below.

I walk around the side of the apartment building to the garden I planted. When we'd arrived, the dirt patch had been overrun by weeds. "I could tend to it," I suggested. "Make the place come back to life a little."

"A fine idea," Papa said quickly. Gardening, if done properly without too much strain, is an acceptable avocation for women. "Though we're hardly likely to be here long enough to see things grow."

"Then it will be here for others," I replied stubbornly. I'd planted flowers, tulips and other perennials that I hoped would blossom for years even after we were gone, something beautiful to leave behind. One of the plants has fallen, I notice. I dig my hands deep into the soil, savoring the buried warmth. Then I stand too quickly, my hands creating a smear of dirt across my dress.

I make my way down the cobblestone lane in the opposite direction from the crowds at the hotel, in case Papa is watching out the window. I head toward the market, skirting the edge of the park that sits at the end of the street. I have come to know the quiet rhythm of this part of the town through my days here—the old woman who sits at the corner with her poodle as if waiting for a bus that will not come, the two men who appear every morning at seven to slip schnapps into their coffees and sit wordlessly for twenty minutes before getting up and going in opposite directions. Are they brothers, cousins, friends? Was their routine always like this or was it disrupted during the war?

Gazing down the path into the park, I am reminded of Krysia. I've not seen her since we came out here. Versailles is at least twenty-five kilometers away from Paris, too far for an impromptu excursion into the city.

Stopping short of the market, where most of the stalls are indeed closed, I double back around the block to the hotel. The crowd has thickened now, a low murmur of expectancy crackling through the onlookers. Moments later, three buses appear on the road, old coaches belching smoke and making such noise that it seems questionable whether they will make the last ten meters of the trip. A truck rides ahead of the buses. It lurches to a stop then dumps a bunch of boxes in the hotel courtyard as unceremoniously as though they are garbage. Studying closer, I can see that it is luggage, once-fine suitcases now covered with dust and grime.

The bus doors open and the German delegation begins to emerge. They are bureaucrats, stooped older men, thin and paunched, bald and bearded, indistinguishable from the other nations' delegates, but for their low shoulders and downcast eyes. They shuffle forward to face the indignity of sorting through the luggage, each to find and carry his own.

A boy lets forth a jeer. I brace myself for the rest of the onlookers to join him. Instead, the crowd is silent, their eyes boring into the Germans with pure hatred. Insults would have almost been better. This is why Papa sits at his desk, why he cannot bear to watch. This is not peace or even armistice, but rather the thinnest of truces, scarcely concealing the hatred of the war still bubbling beneath the surface.

A man steps from the last coach behind the others. He is younger, I can tell, even beneath the cloak of his naval coat and hat. Papa had mentioned someone military. My first impression is of a hawk. Steely blue eyes take in the crowd. I'm reminded of the soldiers I saw so often on the Paris streets. Even out of uniform I can spot it—the anxiousness, searching the corners for a cellar or other hiding place, as though the air before him might at any moment explode with grenades and mustard gas.

He starts forward, walking with his shoulders squared,

seeming to clear the path ahead of him as he goes. Then his head lifts slightly and his eyes flick in my direction and I can swear, though I am one in a crowd of hundreds, he is looking directly at me.

My breath catches. I step back and, as I do, my scarf drops. Suddenly the German breaks from the procession. He steps toward the crowd, which parts. Then he bends down and picks up my scarf and holds it out to me.

I recoil. There is something chilling about him, militaristic and terrifying. Stefan is a soldier, too, I remind myself. But that is different—Stefan is an ordinary man, called into war by circumstances and patriotism. This man is a high-ranking officer, a soldier by nature. I look down, suddenly conscious of the garden dirt on the sleeve of my everyday blouse.

The people around me glare with accusing eyes as if my receipt of this act of kindness somehow makes me complicit. I tilt my head upward but the soldier does not meet my eyes. Should I thank him in German or French? I take the scarf but before I can say anything, the man has rejoined the procession and is gone.

I can hear the party before I can see it, laugher spilling forth down the streets of Neuilly-sur-Seine. We turn the corner and a house in the middle of the street stands as a beacon, light beaming from within. It is not the largest on the block of this affluent Parisian neighborhood, but it gives the impression of being the most grand—flower boxes overflow with blooms too early in the season to be native and great ribbons of silk batting adorn the balconies, as though Armistice Day was last week and not months ago.

I stop midstreet, drawing my flimsy shawl against the evening, which is pleasant but chilly enough to remind me that it is not summer yet. Normally I would have dreaded such an affair. But after weeks locked away in dreary Versailles, I somehow welcome the return to the city and its bustle, even with Tante Celia as my host. There is no room in Versailles for Celia, a woman without official status, so she has remained behind in Paris. Papa is lonely for her, I can tell, by his quieter than usual demeanor, the excuses he has found to stay over in the city after dinners.

Celia touches my elbow as we climb the stairs. "You've heard of Elsa Maxwell, *n'est-ce pas?*" She jumps indiscriminately between German and French.

"Of course." I reply in German, not bothering to lower my voice. It's not as if anybody will be fooled into believing we are someone else. Elsa Maxwell is ubiquitous. A reporter in the softest sense of the word, she is in fact a social doyenne whose real fame came from hosting soirees such as this. "She threw parties in London during the war." I neglect to mention that I had not been to any of them.

Inside, the house is hot as August, too many bodies pressed close, trying to move in all directions. The party has been going on for hours, the festive atmosphere a train we had missed. A far cry from the stuffy receptions I had attended with Papa, there is no pretense of restraint. The men have loosened or in some cases removed their ties. The women have kicked off their shoes and those who have not bobbed their hair have let it loose from its pins. The women who had come to Paris were of an unusual sort—would-be writers and entertainers and journalists whose free-spirited nature surely gave consternation to the wives who had been left at home. Their dresses are the latest fashions, Oriental-themed shifts, Bohemian frocks without any pretense of a corset. I feel positively frumpy in my staid rose party dress, though not as much so as Celia, who with her high collar and crinolines stands out like a peacock, or a jester in an Elizabethan play.

Bodies fill the makeshift dance floor in the center of the great room, moving in strange new ways to the lively jazz music that blares from a gramophone. Two women dance as though one was a man, pressed close together. A strange scent, something strong like burning flowers, mixes with the faint odor of sweat in the air. There is a kind of desperation to the revelry, especially among the women. It is more than just the wiping away of cobwebs and sorrow of a world struggling to live again. The chance for a normal life with a husband and children has been denied to so many, a generation of would-be suitors gone to the trenches. The men who were left were the oddities, those who had escaped the military for some sort of infirmity, and those like Stefan who came back broken.

"All of this immorality," Celia remarks in French, "Everyone's roles confused, the lines between men and women gone, brought about by women going into work."

"You really think that's the cause of all of this?" My voice is incredulous. "There are so many other reasons. What about the desperation of the war, not to mention the influx of large numbers of soldiers now with too much time on their hands, so far from home?" Celia sniffs, unpersuaded.

"It's a sight, isn't it?" a woman next to me remarks idly. I nod, my eyes traveling toward the dance floor where the two women are locked together now, nearly kissing. There is something about being in Paris here, away from familial and societal expectations back home, that has given people license to act this way. "Austrians at the party, as if they were our friends," she adds. I step back, stung. The woman had not been referring to the outlandish behavior at all, but was incensed by our kind being here, the enemy treated as equals.

"Come." I follow Celia through the packed room. She disappears into the crowd ahead of me and, after searching above the sea of heads in vain, I give up trying to keep up and instead make my way to one of the open windows. The cold, crisp air is a welcome relief against my face, a reprieve from the swaths of perfumed smoke.

Outside a woman in a tattered work dress picks through the rubbish in the alley adjacent to the house. Though the homeless have become an increasingly common sight in Paris, I am taken aback by the woman, not much older than myself, searching the garbage for food. What does she think of us being here with all of our parties and revelry and noise? I imagine a husband taken at the front, hungry children back home. Sensing me, she looks up and her eyes widen with alarm, fearful that I will reproach or report her for being there. Desperately I reach into my purse and fling coins through the window, ashamed by the callousness of the gesture, as well as the inadequacy of my aid.

Celia is at my arm again, this time with our hostess, a buxom woman with short brown hair and a broad smile I recognize from the society pages of the newspaper. "Elsa, you remember…" I hold my breath, waiting for the woman to deny our having met in London.

But Elsa Maxwell, accustomed to traveling in wide circles and knowing people less often than she is known, sweeps me into a firm hug that has none of the airiness of the kisses so often exchanged here. "Darling!" Celia watches, eyes wide, apparently having bought the subterfuge. Elsa releases me. "If you'll excuse me, I must get everyone started on the game."

"Game?" But she has already moved on, leaving a burst of Chanel in her wake.

A moment later a bell rings and Elsa appears on the landing of the broad staircase in the middle of the foyer, commanding a presence well beyond what her rather plain appearance suggests. The din in the room instantly dulls, but there is still too much noise for me to hear well. She makes an announcement, holding up papers of some sort. A whisper of excitement blows through the crowd. Then she throws the papers into the air with a flourish and they scatter like confetti.

I turn to Tante Celia, confused. "A scavenger game," she exclaims excitedly, scrambling to grab one of the sheets. "It's a treasure hunt," she explains, placing great importance on each syllable.

She scans the paper, then passes it to me. It is a shopping list of the oddest sort: a pair of opera glasses, a man's swimming costume. Some of the items are phrased in riddle. "I don't understand. How are we to buy these things if the shops are closed?"

She titters with superiority, staring toward the door. "We don't buy them. We find them," she replies, gaily as a child. Are we seriously to run around the streets hunting in the darkness?

"I don't…" I start to beg off, following her outside. But Celia has already formed a foursome with two Swedes and together they set off toward the dense trees of the Bois de Boulogne.

As I start toward the massive park, my ankle twists, a sharp but fleeting pain. Celia turns back impatiently. The heel of my shoe, which caught the cobblestone, is cracked and, sensing my moment, I pull intentionally until the heel snaps. "It's broken," I lament, trying to fill my voice with disappointment. "You go on."

Celia hesitates. "If you're sure you'll be fine." Not waiting for my response, she follows the Swedes, who have already run off into the night, intent on the errand of finding a newspaper that is more than a month old. As she disappears into the trees, I sigh. I do not begrudge her excitement when she has so little to call her own. And she would not have left me if I was in real distress.

I limp back toward the house. The party has faded, the salon empty except for a rowdy group of men in the smoking room, a couple kissing shamelessly on one of the settees. I find the butler and ask him to call a taxi.

It is nearly midnight when the cab reaches Versailles. I pay the driver and step out, then peer across the road toward the Hôtel des Réservoirs, where lights still burn on the ground floor despite the late hour. Curious, I walk down the street. In a first-floor library, a man works intensely behind a desk, head low, bathed in yellow light. It is the German naval officer who picked up my scarf. I watch him, transfixed. He looks to be about thirty. He lifts his head and catches my eye, holding my glance for a second longer than he had earlier at the arrival. Then he stands and walks from the room. I step back into the shadows. How rude of me. He obviously minded the intrusion. But then the front door to the hotel opens and I see him silhouetted against the light.

"Can I help you, *mademoiselle?* We are not a zoo."

I flush, seized with the urge to run. "No, of course not." Then I take a step forward, out of the shadows. "It's *fraulein,* actually." I am quick to identify myself as a German out of the earshot of others, as if our kindred citizenship might excuse my watching him. I shift my weight awkwardly to my right foot. "I mean, Margot. Margot Rosenthal."

"The professor's daughter?" I nod. "I'm Georg Richwalder. I'm the military attaché to the delegation."

"I'm sorry if I disturbed you. I broke my heel and was just pausing." I hold up the shoe as evidence, take a step through the gate. He walks down the steps toward me. He is taller than I thought and I crane my neck upward to meet his eyes rather than stare at his chest as we speak.

"May I?"

I hand the shoe to him.

"I can fix this, I think."

I eye him skeptically.

"You learn to be handy in a great many ways when you're at sea. Would you like to come in for some tea while I try?"

I hesitate. The library behind him looks warm and inviting, the quiet and solitude a welcome contrast to the Maxwell party. But it wouldn't be proper. "No, thank you. I'll just be on my way."

"Wait here," he instructs firmly, a man who is used to giving orders. I shiver at his commanding tone. "I'll bring the tools—and some tea—outside."

I sit down on the step. A few minutes later he emerges with two cups of tea and a small kit. "I'm sorry to have disturbed you," I say.

"Not at all." He smiles and in that instant seems not at all the terrifying soldier I'd glimpsed during the delegation's arrival. A chink in the armor. "After so much time on the train, the fresh air is refreshing. The trip was exceedingly long. We sat at one point for eighteen hours for some reason known only to the French." He is wearing the same dark blue uniform as earlier today, but the jacket is unbuttoned, the shirt loosened at the collar.

I run my hand along the step, the stone hard and rough beneath my fingertips. "And the hotel…is it quite dreadful?"

"It's not bad, really. I mean in its heyday I'm sure it was quite grand. But I spent the better part of the four years on a ship, so I may not be the best judge of comfort."

"You were in the navy, weren't you?"

"I was on the *SMS König,* the crown jewel of His Majesty's High Seas Fleet." The pride in his voice is reminiscent of the prewar days, taking me back to the parades down the Unter den Linden, young girls pressing sandwiches and sweets into the hands of newly minted soldiers as they made their way to the station. "Even as a senior officer, my quarters were no bigger than a closet. The hotel has reasonably clean linen and fresh water and I'm not awakened to the sound of gunfire each morning." He smiles. "It's paradise. And the library is wonderful. I shall enjoy working there at night after the rest of the delegation has retired. They're mostly older, and we don't have much in common. But it's not a social occasion."

"And your family—did they mind being left back home?" The question comes out more prying than I intended. "I mean only that I've heard some of the men lamenting that their families couldn't enjoy Paris."

"No." An image pops into my mind of a Frau Richwalder, elegant and well coiffed, keeping the house running back in Germany. "That is, there's no one. I'm not married. Not so much to enjoy here these days, anyway."

"I suppose not." The German delegation was almost entirely confined to the hotel except for sanctioned meetings and a lone excursion.

"There." He hands me my shoe, neatly fixed.

"It's good as new. *Danke*." He watches me, as though lost in thought. Between my mud-streaked dress earlier and broken shoe now, he must think me a wreck.

"Aren't you cold?"

I shake my head stubbornly.

"That's hardly a suitable coat."

"It's the fashion." I struggle to keep the sarcasm from my voice.

"Well, no one is here to see." He takes his coat and puts it around my shoulders in a strange, too-familiar gesture.

A mixture of soap and wool wafts upward from the collar. "Now won't you be cold?"

"I'm something of a polar bear actually. All of those nights on the North Sea."

My eyes travel to the contour of his shoulder, dark against the lighted window. "Papa mentioned that there's a trip to the battlefields scheduled for Sunday. Are you going?"

"Not if I can help it. I've spent the past four years on a battlefield of another sort. I'd like to see them, of course, and pay respects, but on my own, not from the window of a motor coach. I came here to work, not sightsee."

"I suppose you won't be going into Paris for the plenary session tomorrow, either?"

He shook his head. "We weren't asked." How odd, to be summoned all of this distance, only to be sequestered in a hotel, excluded from the very meetings for which you were invited. But then he forces a smile. "It's no matter. So much better to have the time to work and not be shut up in stuffy proceedings all day."

"True. What are you working on?" His eyes widen and I wonder if he minds the question.

"It's quite dry," he says apologetically. He is not offended, just surprised that I might take an interest. "I'm the delegation's military officer and I'm studying plans and proposals as to what the treaty might look at, reading up on what the French and British experts are advocating in order to develop a counter position." He continues, "There's going to be a whole new world, a way for nations to coexist and to form strong alliances that will ensure we never face such de-struction of man like that again." His shoulders straighten. "I can be part of that, I think, by helping the navy to find its place. It's slow going. Not the technical parts—I'm familiar with all of the engineering concepts from the ship. But languages were never my strong point and the delegation can't spare a translator outside of the sessions."

"I can help you," I blurt out, without meaning to. "My French and English are quite good. I've got no technical training but with the aid of a dictionary I could muddle through."

He looks at me dubiously. "It's tremendously dull, lots of engineering reports."

"I studied maths and science through the progymnasium level," I reply. His jaw drops slightly, making his lips even more full. "I know it isn't the typical curriculum for a girl," I add, my words flowing more easily than usual. Back home girls are typically schooled in the gentle arts of music and literature at the high school level. But I had gravitated naturally toward the sciences and Papa had let my curiosity direct my studies.

"There's nothing to be paid for it."

"That's fine."

He coughs slightly. "Then why would you want to?"

"For the chance to do something—" I fumble for the right words, replaying my talks with Krysia "—meaningful. Real." Because I'm sitting here in the middle of the world being formed, I add silently, playing at dinner parties and treasure hunts.

"Fine," he acquiesces. For a moment I am annoyed—

I'm trying to help him, but it sounds as if he is doing me a favor. "It's quite late tonight but if you'd like to come by tomorrow evening at eight, we can work after the delegation retires. You'll need clearance, of course, but that shouldn't be hard to get with your father's credentials."

"So we're agreed."

"*Ja*. If…" he adds, "your father approves."

I bristle and open my mouth to tell him that I am an adult and my own woman. But I can tell by his tone that it is not subject to debate, and that he will not cross another member of the delegation. "I'm sure it will be fine. I will see you tomorrow." I stand and hand him his coat. "Thank you for the shoe, and the tea." He stands. I wait for him to offer to escort me home, but he does not.

Back at the apartment, Papa is hunched over some papers in the study, reading so intensely he does not hear me come in. Smoke curls upward from his pipe, giving off a sickly smell. Seeing me, his brow furrows. "Is something amiss? I thought you were with Celia."

"I was. I came home. Are you working?"

He shakes his head. "Just composing a cable to Uncle Walter." I worry sometimes that Papa reports back to his brother-in-law too much, as if beholden to a superior. But Uncle Walter is just curious, a child being kept from the adults' table, eager for every detail he is missing, as well as an assessment of how the Germans will fare. He has always imagined himself a political thinker. I suspect that in reality he is just an excellent prognosticator of what is to come, and he sorely needs details to do that.

"Papa," I begin tentatively.

"Ja, liebchen?" He looks up and smiles. My father, an absentminded academic, can fairly be accused of spending the better part of life in a hazy bubble of his own thoughts. But he has always had a way of knowing when my tone was serious and required his actual focus and attention.

Which was not the effect I am going for here when I was hoping to pass this by him before he ever had the chance to focus on it. "I've been offered an opportunity to do some work." He raises an eyebrow, and I continue. "Captain Richwalder from the delegation, you know him?"

"The young military officer. We met earlier."

"He needs someone to help him with translations. Please, Papa, I'm just so terribly bored." I don't tell him that the work will need to happen in the evening or in the library of the hotel. "I just want to help."

He rubs his chin. "I see no harm in it. It will be good for your linguistic skills." He turns back to his papers.

Dismissed, I walk to my room. Across the road, the massive expanse of the palace grounds, trees and fountains are shrouded in darkness. I press my head against the window, craning my neck to glimpse the hotel. The light in the library still burns yellow on the first floor and I imagine Captain Richwalder hunched over his papers. I wonder what the work will be like. Will my language skills be sufficient? Remembering his imposing gaze, I shiver. Then, I turn off the light and climb into bed, anticipating with excitement and more than a little dread the day that is to come.

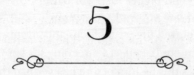

5

It is just shy of eight o'clock and the lamps glow behind the curtains at the hotel as I approach. I knock and a few seconds later the door opens. Captain Richwalder wears no jacket this evening, but his dress shirt is pressed crisply, the short hair above his ears still damp from washing. "Thank you for being prompt," he says, sounding as though used to people being otherwise. I had, in fact, loitered a good twenty minutes at our apartment, not wanting to arrive too early, checking my reflection with more care than I otherwise would have to make sure I look capable. My clothes are simple, a starched cream blouse with a scalloped collar and a navy skirt a shade longer than is fashionable these days.

Taking in his stiff, formal demeanor, I am suddenly uneasy. What if he is difficult to work for, even unkind? Though I volunteered to do this and am not receiving pay, Papa will expect me to honor the commitment I've made and see the job through.

Captain Richwalder leads me through the lobby of the hotel, which is nicer than I might have expected from the drab exterior. The maroon curtains are just a bit faded and the chandelier overhead is every bit as elaborate as the one in our Paris hotel. He opens the door to the study. "Please make yourself at home. I'll just be a moment." As he closes the door behind him, I remove my coat. The library is modest in size, no bigger than our parlor down the street, but pleasant, with soft, overstuffed chairs and book-filled shelves that climb to the ceiling. The air carries the same damp, musty smell that permeates most of the town.

Captain Richwalder returns a moment later with two cups of tea and sets them down on the low table. "It's a bit warmer now. The weather, I mean." His attempt to make small talk is awkward, simple conversation strange on his tongue.

"Indeed." I smooth my hair, which is pulled back in a loose, low knot. Then I decide to be direct. "So what is it that you need me to do?"

His face relaxes at being given permission to turn to work and he motions for me to follow him over to the desk in the corner, where he holds the chair out for me to sit. "There are a number of military matters related to the peace treaty that are to be proposed, and I've been asked to work on those, not surprisingly, that involve the navy. The Imperial Navy is one of the finest in the world," he adds, unable to keep a note of pride from his voice. Or was, I cannot help but think. "And I believe there's a real role for the navy as a peacekeeper in the new world order."

His suggestion is the first I've heard of such an idea. "Do you think that's what the Allies have in mind?"

"Surely some sort of partnership. Remember what Wilson said at the cease-fire, peace without blame." It was true that in the desperate efforts to stop the fighting, Wilson had made such hasty promises. But the rhetoric since we've been in Paris has been far more pointed.

He continues. "So I believe such an arrangement is possible. But we've got to make the case." He is animated now, gesturing broadly with his hands to illustrate his point. "There's a vast amount of correspondence about the role that naval fleets might play, drawn up before and during the war. Synthesizing it will give a sense of what the Big Four are thinking and help to frame any proposal. But we have to work quickly."

I nod. The other nations have been meeting for close to six months, inviting the German delegation only at the final hour. Captain Richwalder's idea makes sense, but the window for providing any sort of input and making a difference is slim. "I would have started earlier, of course, but I was given access to the materials just days before leaving Berlin," he adds.

"Of course."

"I've prioritized the documents most in need of translation." He spreads the papers out on the desk before me. I would have expected the hands of a soldier, thick and crude. But his fingers are long, more artist than warrior, delicate half-moons at the cuticle.

He retreats to one of the chairs by the low table, which is piled high with papers, and I turn to the first document. It is a report on the structure of the smaller vessel fleets, and though once or twice I consult the dictionary I brought with me, to be certain of the exact words, it is not altogether difficult. My translation settles into an easy rhythm.

Working alongside Captain Richwalder is not so different than reading in the study with Papa.

When I've finished the first page, I glance up, studying Captain Richwalder out of the corner of my eye. He is as imposing as he'd appeared at the arrival ceremony, with strong features seemingly etched from granite. But close up, there are little things I can see now—long eyelashes, almost impossibly so for a man, a bottom lip much fuller than the top. Faint, end-of-day stubble covers his cheeks.

He looks up unexpectedly. "Do you need something?"

"No." Heat rises from my neck as I fumble to find an excuse for my staring. "I was just wondering, how are things in Berlin?"

"You've not been back?"

"Not since the start of the war. We were in England."

"England?"

"Yes, Papa was on a teaching fellowship." My own explanation sounds uneasy. At the time, our departure had been too rushed to ask. But afterward I had questioned it silently myself: Why had we gone to an enemy country right after the war broke out? Papa could have postponed the fellowship. But there had been an urgency to our leaving. Had he been worried for our safety? The war never reached German soil, and surely at Uncle Walter's palatial mansion in the countryside we would have been fine. Had he been afraid of something else?

Captain Richwalder shakes his head. "Very bad, I'm afraid," he says, returning to my original question. "The Social Democrats nominally hold power in Berlin, but the south, Bavaria especially, has become a hotbed of communist activity. There are rumors that the government may have to retake Munich by force to restore order."

"That I've read in the press. But what is it like on the street?"

He pauses, struggling to fashion a description beyond the political. "Strikes, protests, rioting. Neighbors who lived in peace their whole lives taking sides and fighting one another. It's anarchy. You will find the city much changed. Immigrants have poured in by the thousands from the east, living in these cramped apartments, entire families in a single room. And there's no food, not for them and not for the people with money to buy it. The war is over, yet women and children continue to starve because of the blockade." His tone is harsh.

"Oh!" I bring my hand to my mouth. I hadn't understood it until then. Removed from the continent, safely tucked away in England, war seemed a remote thing, fought in the trenches by men who were strong enough to withstand it. Maybe that's why Papa accepted the appointment in England. He must have sensed the horror of what was to come and wanted to spare me. While I was bemoaning the rainy British weather and lack of things to do, people back home were dying from hunger and cold. I shudder. "Your description of the chaos makes it sound like Russia."

"Perhaps, but I don't think it's going to go that way. The SDP is so divided within that they can't organize to get anything done, much less form an effective government. The right is taking advantage of that, capitalizing on all of the anger—they've managed to convince lots of people who weren't there that the new government was responsible for our ultimate defeat in the war. It's not true, of course, but people back home don't know that and it makes for an attractive, simple story. So the right has some popular appeal but they don't have the numbers. Things will settle somewhere in the middle. It's terribly dissatisfying."

"Maybe." To me, there is a kind of comfort in the inertia, a safeguard against any one extreme taking too much.

He picks up one of the cups of tea from the low table and walks over. Our fingers brush as he hands it to me. "Forgive my bluntness. All of the time on the ship has made me forget how to speak to a lady properly."

"Not at all. I much prefer plain speech." I take a sip of tea, then set the cup down well away from the papers. "Captain Richwalder…"

"Georg," he interjects. "If you don't mind."

"Georg," I say, the name unfamiliar and awkward on my tongue. "What will you do after the conference?"

He retreats to his chair, stretches his legs out before him. "Return to the battleship, I suppose, or a different craft if that was needed."

"You haven't seen enough of war?"

"There is no peace without war," Georg says. "There's a concept in Asia called yin-yang, two opposite halves of the whole. War and peace are just that. And soldiers are needed. Without the military, there would be no order."

I want to protest that man's nature would allow him to coexist peacefully, but I know that he is right. "I mean, what would you do if you couldn't go back to a battleship?" I ask, shifting topics slightly.

Georg cocks his head, as though he had not before contemplated the question. He had always assumed that there would be a navy and a place for him in it.

"Would you join the new government?"

He shakes his head. "I've got no patience for bureaucracy, and the capital makes me feel as though the walls and buildings are closing in around me. No, I'd probably return to Hamburg and oversee the family shipping business. If I can't be on the sea, at least I could be near it."

"Your family ships goods?"

"No, we build ships." I had not realized until now that Georg is wealthy. I've always been oblivious to matters of money and class—too oblivious, Tante Celia remarked once. But with his uniform and haircut, it would have been impossible to tell. "There isn't much of a 'we' anymore, unfortunately. My parents both died some time ago, and my brother Peter was killed at the Battle of Jutland."

"How terrible."

"He was on a ship not far from mine that was torpedoed. I saw him go down and I could do nothing to stop it." His recounting is factual and precise, but his eyes cloud over at the memory. "Eight ships and nine thousand men at that battle alone. We joined the navy together, but it was really more his dream to be a great naval officer. I just went along."

Now Georg had picked up the mantle, fulfilling the career his brother could never have. "Tell me more about Hamburg," I say, trying to gently steer the subject away from war. The sadness on his normally strong face is somehow unbearable.

But he will not be dissuaded. "I think Peter wanted to

escape to the sea. You see, our parents were terribly strict and they had such high expectations."

"Yes, of course." I nod.

"I have a sister, too. My parents had plans for her to marry someone rich and fairly dreadful, so she ran away to Austria. She lives in a cottage in the Obersalzberg with her husband, someone she actually wanted, cared for, and they have about a dozen children. I see her occasionally, send money. They have a modest lifestyle but it's very happy."

"And noisy, I'm sure, with all of those children," I remark.

"I don't mind," he replies, surprising me. Quiet and order seem better suited to him. "I would have liked children."

"You talk like you're eighty!" I exclaim. "You can still have them."

"I'm twenty-five," Georg replies. "I will be twenty-six, tomorrow, in fact." There is something grave and imposing about his demeanor that makes him appear more than just a few years older.

"There's still plenty of time." Though it is not at all hot in the room, my skin feels suddenly moist.

"I suppose. And you?"

"I do want children," I reply with more certainty than I'd planned. It was not something I'd thought about on a conscious level until now.

"No, I was asking about your family. Are there many of you?"

"Oh." For the second time in an hour, I feel myself blush. "A small family, also. Just Papa and me." I do not count

Tante Celia or our other extended relations. "My mother died of flu when I was younger."

"I'm sorry." His voice is full with the empathy of shared loss.

"Growing up an only child, Papa working all of the time, was sometimes a lonely existence. That's why I'd like to have children. How many, I don't know, but definitely more than one." I feel myself talking too fast and saying too much. I have not felt this comfortable speaking with anyone since Krysia. "With siblings you always have each other…" I stop, realizing my error. Georg had his brother until he died at war, in front of his very eyes.

But he does not take offense. "I understand what you mean. My sister, Alice, is my dearest friend, though I don't see her that often."

"And you, do you get lonely?"

He shook his head. "There was a time when Peter was gone, and my parents, too, that I didn't want to go on. But I've made my peace with it now." Solitude had become his default state, such that he did not know how to be otherwise.

"There are so many things I want to do before having children."

"Like what?"

"Well, travel mostly. Not just England and France, but the whole world. Africa, maybe. Or take that railway that's been constructed to China." I'd thought about it so often since my conversations with Krysia a few months earlier. Talking about it now with Georg, the fantasy journeys I've constructed in my head feel almost possible.

"The Trans-Siberian?" He chuckles as though the idea is far-fetched.

"No, really. I want to see the world, not just the cities, but the edges and frontiers before they are developed and changed into looking just like everywhere else."

"Then you would have loved the navy. I've been to some of the places you mentioned—Japan, for one. But I've never been far from harbor to the really deep inland bits." Georg has seen great swaths of the world but always from a great distance, just scratching the surface. But I want to delve deeply into such places—to see the children walking to school and the way the people eat, how they live. "There's nothing better than standing on the deck of the ship as the coast disappears behind you, a clear horizon ahead." A dreamy, faraway look comes into Georg's eyes. "Do you enjoy the seaside?"

"No. I fear the water," I confess. Growing up in land-locked Berlin, I had not seen the ocean until I was six, when we'd taken a holiday to the Dutch seaside during Papa's visitorship at Leiden. I found the dark, murky waters and the rough, churning current unsettling. Since then, I've had terrible nightmares about it—a giant wave rising and swallowing me whole. On the ferry crossing I stayed inside the cabin, reading a book, pretending I was elsewhere and trying not to see the endless water that surrounded us on all sides. "It just feels so ominous." I'm not sure why I'm sharing this confession with a man I barely know.

He looks puzzled, as if the idea of someone not liking the water is unfathomable. "Can you swim?"

"I don't think so. I've never tried."

"I could make you love the water." An image flashes through my mind of Georg and I on a seaside promenade. The cool sea breeze and taste of salt air almost seem real. "Or at least not to be afraid. The thing is to understand that it is a different world—we are visitors in the ocean, not in charge of it. So you have to treat it with respect, come to learn the local customs, so to speak." His words make sense. But I doubt that I could ever love it as he does, or even be comfortable.

"Of course, being on a sailboat is one thing. A naval fighting ship is quite another." He cringes as the memories press over him. "You should give the ocean another chance. It's the only place to really be free," he adds.

"I don't know about that. The mountains can be most liberating." Papa and I have always taken our holidays in the Alps. We would pack simple cheese and fruit that would keep for a day, setting off into the woods as the sun broke. We might not speak for hours, each lost in our own thoughts as we wound between the trees. It was a kind of quiet meditation and a peace I'd not found elsewhere.

I'd suggested hiking when we were in England. "We could go north to the Lakes." But Papa had shaken his head. "Two Germans disappearing into the middle of nowhere might provoke suspicion." And anger. There were stories of a mob beating up a few German expatriates in Leeds just as the war had broken out. Papa insisted that we stay in the cities where help was available and we would not be isolated, protested every time I went out alone.

"Margot…" It is the first time Georg has used my name. "Yes?"

But before he can continue, there is a creaking sound and the library door, already ajar, opens farther. Papa stands there in his overcoat. I look at the clock. It is nearly ten. Georg and I have talked for most of the time and I've scarcely done any work. "I'm sorry to interrupt, but I'm headed home and I thought that perhaps I could escort you." I smile inwardly. Papa is nowhere near finished work— midnight is only a starting point for him. But he was concerned enough about my being with Georg to break from what he was doing and come to check on me.

"I'm fine, Papa. Though..." I turn to Georg. "I'm afraid we didn't get very far."

Georg nods with recognition. "It's no matter. We can resume tomorrow."

"Same time?"

"I should be most grateful." He turns to Papa. "I trust you'll be at Ambassador Bossart's dinner party Friday?" Papa had mentioned the dinner in passing, a rare occasion for the German delegation to leave the confines of the hotel and enjoy dinner in the city as a show of good faith.

Papa smiles wryly. "Is there any choice?" The men chuckle, bonding over their shared dislike for social obligations and their preference for solitary work.

"Good night, Captain." Though he has bade me to call him by his given name, doing so feels too intimate in front of Papa.

"An odd chap," Papa remarks when we are well clear of the hotel. "So quiet." His description does not sound at all like Georg, who chatted so easily we scarcely made it through any of the translation. But I think back to how scary and imposing he seemed the day the Germans arrived. Knowing him now, it is hard to picture him as the same person. "Some say he's a bit touched in the head."

"He's not," I protest, too defensive of the man I've only just met. "I mean, perhaps he's a bit shaky from battle, but otherwise he appears quite normal." How can Papa and I look at the exact same man and see such different things?

We cross the street to our apartment building, not speaking as we walk up the stairs. "Make sure you don't stay up too late tonight," Papa cautions as he unlocks the door to the flat. "Tante Celia rang that your appointment tomorrow is at nine, which means you'll need to be on the seven-forty train."

"Appointment?" The dress shop, I remember. My wedding gown is ready for its first fitting. I do not want to go, and consider rescheduling. But best not to make waves—it is a gift I've always had, knowing when to go with the current and stifle my rebellious impulses. "The little diplomat," Papa joked, more than once. "Oh, yes, the fitting." Going into Paris will give me an excuse to visit Krysia, as well. I've missed her mightily since our move. "Good night, Papa."

In my room, I change into a nightgown and robe, then pull back the drapes. I strain to glimpse across the road, pressing my head against the window frame. The light in the hotel library still burns. Georg. Though I cannot see him, I imagine him hunched over the desk, studying one of his reports. He so believes in what he is doing, the ability to make a difference and convince the Allies that there is a place for us in this new world order. I hope, for his sake as well as for Germany's, that he is right.

There is a knock at my door and I jump back from the window. "Yes, Papa?"

"I'd almost forgotten. A letter came for you." My stomach sinks as I take the envelope. Another missive from Stefan, no doubt, when I still had not answered the last. But if it was from Stefan, Papa would have said as much. Instead, he looks quizzically at the blocky, unfamiliar script on the coarse brown envelope. When I do not answer, he hands it to me and leaves with a slight shrug, unwilling to pry.

I drop to the edge of the bed and turn the envelope over, suddenly uneasy. Then, too curious to hold back, I rip it open.

Please come see me about a matter of utmost importance.

It is signed by Ignatz Stein.

6

"Turn to the left, if you please," the dressmaker says. I shift, cringing as the stiff material scratches against my skin.

"Perhaps just a bit more lace at the neck," Tante Celia offers, rising from her chair and squinting with an appraising eye. Inwardly, I groan. The too-tight collar already creeps against my chin, making me want to gag.

"I don't know…" I demur.

"Your mother," Celia replies firmly, "would have loved the lace."

I open my mouth to protest. The woman in the photos was natural and soft, her flowing clothes nothing like the elaborate frocks Celia favors. I am quite sure she would have preferred my gown to be simple. But the argument is pointless. Celia invokes my mother's memory frequently as both shield and sword, and my own vague recollections of her provide little ammunition for countering Celia's assertions.

As the seamstress pins the fabric around my waist, I see my reflection behind her in the wide mirror. The solemn, dark-haired woman in the white dress seems a stranger. Behind me, Celia's image appears. My aunt is immaculately coiffed as ever, her hair in a flawless chignon. But the latest fashions cannot mask her too-weak chin and wide nose.

Celia has always been about the appearance of things, as if she is trying to plaster over the imperfections and defects of her life, like the man that can never quite be hers because his heart still belongs to her beautiful, dead sister.

An hour earlier, I'd followed Tante Celia reluctantly into the boutique, which was tucked on a side street in the Faubourg Saint-Honoré district, eyeing the satin-and-tulle-clad mannequins with unbridled dread. I imagined then the weddings those dresses represent, the breathless anticipation of a shared future. Would it be different if I was excited about the prospect of marriage and was picking a dress of my own accord, unfettered by the expectations of others?

Expectations. My thoughts turn to the note from Ignatz Stein. What could he possibly want from me? He could not be hoping, these many months later, that I might convey some information to him about Papa's work. I should go to see him today while I am in the city and find out. I shiver, seeing his dark eyes. "Be still, please," the seamstress admonishes.

I stand motionless for what seems like forever, feeling the seamstress's soft rustling hands as she pins the bottom. Finally, she is finished and, with Celia's help, carefully extricates me from the dress. "Are you hungry?" Celia asks a few minutes later as we step onto the street of grand shops, their wide-paned windows displaying jewelry and furs and fine silks that no one can afford anymore. I inhale deeply, clearing the stuffiness of the dress shop from my lungs. "We could go to the food hall at the department store," she offers.

I hesitate, then nod. I am eager to try to see Krysia while I am in the city. But Celia's expression is so hopeful I cannot refuse. And I am hungry, having not eaten this morning at Celia's behest in order to remain as slim as possible for the fitting.

We make our way down the boulevard des Capucines with its rows of fashionable stores and restaurants, past the newspaper kiosks and the stalls selling fruit. Spring has broken in earnest, the trees that line the pavement in full bloom, crocuses sprouting purple from the flower beds. The outdoor cafés overflow with patrons, women in fresh spring fashions and men in blazers with carnations in their lapels. They spill from the tables onto the sidewalks, making it difficult to pass. Above, every shutter in the city has been flung open to let in the fresh air.

Soon we reach the Galeries Lafayette, its grand staircase and glass dome more reminiscent of an opera house than a department store. The ground-floor food hall appears much like I remember it before the war, but the space is too big for the goods that are now available. There is a subtle pride to the way the sellers have laid out the breads, and a reverence with which the shoppers accept their parcels of food that suggest the years of hunger and doing without will not be easily forgotten. "Not so many vegetables," Tante Celia remarks critically. I cringe at the obviousness of her German accent.

"Perhaps when the fields can be tilled with fertilizer instead of the blood of Frenchmen," a woman beside us replies haughtily, then turns away. Suddenly I am not hungry.

Tante Celia lifts her chin with surprising defiance. "Why don't you find us a table?" she suggests to me.

I navigate my way through the crowd toward the seating

area. *"Pardon,"* I say as a man bumps into me. I step aside to let him pass. But he brushes against me again, this time pushing me toward the wall. The assault was intentional, I realize, as I look up into the face of Ignatz Stein.

He removes his brown fedora and tips it in my direction. "Hello, Margot," he says, and there is something predatory about his tone. He looks strangely out of place away from the café.

"Monsieur Stein…" I lick my lips uneasily. "This is a coincidence."

"You didn't answer my note."

"I only received it late last night. There was hardly time."

He clucks his tongue. "I understand. Fittings and parties and all. It's a busy life."

He must have followed me, but why? I decide to ignore his sarcasm. "What is it that you want?"

"You had said you would keep your eyes open." No longer the affable café proprietor, he looms over me, menacing.

"I've not seen or heard anything from my father that might be of interest." I fumble for an explanation. "We're so much more removed from everything since moving out to Versailles."

"But you're working for the German officer now, aren't you?"

How had he known? It was a development not two days old, so recent I'd not even had time to tell Krysia. "That should prove useful," he continues, not bothering to wait for me to confirm. "Information about German military operations is scarce and valuable."

I raise my hand. "I have no interest…"

"Pity, isn't it, about Cottin? Poor fool really thought he could stop Clemenceau from voting against his beloved Greater Serbia. One only hopes he can be persuaded to remain silent…" Ignatz knows that I will do anything to protect the truth about Cottin's source, to keep the blame from falling to Papa.

I stare up at him with revulsion. Stein is Jewish, too, but he is a crude caricature, greedy and manipulative, the way the anti-Semites would paint us all. "If it is a question of money…" I don't know why I have said this. I have none of my own, but I could figure out something.

"Don't insult us. We don't want money from you or any of the bourgeoisie scum." He spits this last word. "Your contacts and position make you far more valuable to us than any compensation."

I open my mouth to protest—I cannot possibly steal from Georg. Then, thinking of Papa, my shoulders slump. "What is it you want me to do?"

He drops his voice. "The Germans have claimed they've demilitarized." I stare at him in disbelief. We've scarcely begun to recover from the war—how could Ignatz possibly be contemplating another one already? I recall uneasily Georg's insistence the previous night that a strong military is essential for peace. Perhaps Ignatz is not that far off. He continues, "We believe they've stockpiled munitions in the east—and those could be used to support the Whites in their fight against Lenin and the Bolsheviks. Keep an eye out for anything about the German military plans, particularly those on the Eastern Front. Reports, cables—get copies if you can."

"Who is the work for?" I press. "Really, if I'm to risk things and help…"

"A small group of us gather information to help counter the fascist influence back home. The head of the group is known covertly as Red Thorn."

"Can I meet him?"

"I'm afraid not. Just deliver the papers to me."

But before I can protest, Tante Celia is at my side. "Is something wrong?" I turn back toward Ignatz, but he is already crossing the hall, enveloped by the crowd. "Who was that odd man?"

"A friend of Krysia's. I was asking after her."

"Oh, the Polish woman," Celia's tone was dismissive, as if talking about one of the maids. "The pianist."

"You've heard of her?" For once, I am almost impressed.

"Of course. Anyone who is anyone has Krysia Smok play at their party, and her husband Marcin, too, if one can get him." To Celia, Krysia is a commodity and a sign of status, not a person.

"She's the daughter of an ambassador, actually," I reply, fighting to keep the annoyance from my voice.

Her expression remains skeptical. "This is Paris. Anyone can reinvent themselves here."

A waiter brings the tray of assorted cheeses Celia had selected to one of the tables and I take a cracker. "So, I was thinking of salmon terrines for the starter course," Celia says, turning to the wedding menu as though we were in the middle of a conversation about it. No one is more excited about my engagement than Celia. Though they had fallen on hard times of late, the Osters are an old Berlin family and the fact that they are socially well-placed made Stefan a palatable choice in Celia's eyes. And it is the wedding she never had the chance to plan for herself. I nod as she continues speaking, still shaken by my encounter with Ignatz and what he has asked me to do.

"Would you like to go shopping?" she asks when we've finished eating. "The boutique over on rue Fleury has re-opened. Or shall I just have the car take us back?" *Us.* She has no reason to come to Versailles. Escorting me back to the suburb is merely a pretense to wait and see Papa.

"Actually, I'd like to go see a friend," I reply. "Here in the city."

"The Polish woman?" Her nose wrinkles as she tries to comprehend my preference for spending time with Krysia over her. "Suit yourself," she says quickly.

Celia's jealous. For years, she has been trying to be some sort of surrogate for my mother, an older sister perhaps. Celia is closer to my age than my mother's. We might have been friends, if only we shared some mutual interest or concern beyond Papa. But then Krysia came along and our friendship was instantaneous. I'm not trying to be callous with Celia's feelings. Who can explain why we bond so readily with one person but not another? It is human nature, some odd makeup of our biology perhaps, or a sense that we were destined to be with some people.

Celia really tries to be there, though, not just for Papa but for me, in a hundred little ways that are missing without my mother. I am so ungrateful. "I'll come in next week and we can go shopping then," I offer. Her face brightens.

Twenty minutes later, I step out of a cab at Krysia's. Perhaps I should have called ahead. But she had said Poles did not mind drop-in guests. I ring the bell.

"You again," she says teasingly when I reach the top-floor landing, kissing me airily on both cheeks. She wears a gauzy blouse, flat laced slippers that give the impression of a ballerina. "I haven't seen you at any of the salons."

"I've been working." It had not occurred to me that Krysia might wonder about my absence the way I once had hers.

Behind her there is a shuffling noise and a man appears in the doorway. "You must be Margot."

Krysia's husband looks nothing like I might have expected of a world-renowned musician. In sharp contrast to the brooding artists I'd met at the café, Marcin has a wide grin that lifts his pink, cherubic cheeks close to his eyes. He is a good foot shorter than Krysia, with a full stomach and salt-and-pepper hair, a premature gray. Somewhere between playing Saint Nicholas, if he'd been a bit taller, and one of the elves.

I flush, flattered that Krysia had spoken about me. What had she said? "I hope I'm not intruding."

"It's fine," Krysia says. "Marcin was just leaving."

And whether that is true or said out of politeness, Marcin picks up his coat. "Goodbye, my love." Marcin's expression leaves no doubt as to his adoration for Krysia.

She gazes at Marcin and there is a softness to her eyes that I have not seen before. Her attachment to her husband is not a contradiction to the independent woman I've come to know. Marcin's love supports her and gives her that strength. He is clearly devoted, but yet she still seems so alone. It's the child who has left a hollow place within her that can never be filled.

"So you've found something to occupy your time?" Krysia asks when the door has closed. She pours two cups of coffee, brings them to the settee.

I sit down. Sunlight streams in through the lace curtains, creating dancing patterns of shadows on the parquet floors. "I'm just translating some documents for the delegation." It goes without saying that I am referring to the Germans, and I study her face. Will she be offended that I am helping them? "It's hardly a life makeover, I suppose." My tone is apologetic now.

"But it's a start."

"Perhaps. Only…" Picturing Ignatz looming above me in the food hall, my stomach twists. "You remember the attempt on Clemenceau's life?"

She nods. "That idiot Cottin thought he was helping his cause. Instead he just gave those in power an excuse to be less benevolent."

"Oh, Krysia!" Suddenly I am telling her everything about Stein's request that I look for information, first from Papa and now Georg, his threat to expose the truth if I did not. "I'm so sorry I didn't say anything earlier. But I didn't know what to do. He was your friend and so I thought…"

"He put you in a very difficult position and that was wrong." Her lips set grimly. "I long suspected that Stein was up to something. He's a wild card—he lost his parents in Kiev pogroms as a child, made his way on his wits since he was nine years old." She takes a sip of coffee, gazing out the window. "The war produced all sorts of would-be spies like Stein. Intelligence is everywhere. All of the information that was once locked up in vaults at ministries is now out, making it that much more enticing for opportunists and rogues." Suddenly I see a whole underworld to the conference. "Most likely he's just acting on his own, like Cottin."

My hope rises. "Do you really think so?"

"Let me make some inquiries and find out if there's something to be done about it all."

"You have contacts?"

"Nothing personal, of course. But I've got a cousin who is involved with the Cheka."

Cheka is the intelligence arm of the communist party, rumored to be operating on behalf of Russia throughout Europe. I shudder at the notion, foreign and ominous. Somehow, though, it does not surprise me that Krysia has connections everywhere. "You won't tell Ignatz that we've spoken?"

"No, of course not."

"If something should happen to implicate Papa, I couldn't bear it." My voice is pleading now. "He's in a terrible position as it is, suspected by the Allies because he is German, and by the Germans because he is a Jew."

"What about you? Do you consider yourself Jewish German or a German Jew?" she asks.

I tilt my head, puzzled. "I'm both," I insist. I've certainly never felt as though I had to choose.

"Marcin is Jewish," she informs me.

"Oh." Gentle and refined, he is nothing like Ignatz or the other Jews I've seen from Poland and other places to the east. And he is married to a Gentile. Though we live among our non-Jewish neighbors and see them socially and do business with them, intermarriage is just not something that happens.

"His family has not spoken to us since the wedding." Her lower lip droops, pulling her whole face downward.

"I'm sorry."

"It's a hard thing to be rejected simply for being who you are." She laughs. "There are a great many reasons to dislike me, but usually people at least meet me first."

"Nonsense." To me, Krysia is wonderful, mysterious and sure of herself. But there is something about her quiet confidence, the way she challenges people, that could be off-putting.

"Anyway, I'll take care of Stein," she says, patting my hand. "Try not to think too much about it." Her tone is so reassuring that for a moment I almost believe she is right.

By the time the train pulls into Versailles, it is nearly dark. I'd lingered longer than I had intended at Krysia's and there is no time to go back to the apartment to freshen and comb the dust from my hair before I have to be at work. As I near the hotel, my step quickens. Georg is waiting by the door when I arrive. Warmth rises in me, and I am more glad than I should have been to see him again. "I'm sorry if I'm late," I apologize. "I had an errand in the city and..."

"Not at all. The library's not available this evening, I'm afraid. It's being cleaned. But I've cleared a spot in my rooms for you to work." Pushing a vision of Papa's disapproving stare from my mind, I follow him down the corridor. He unlocks the door and lets me into a small sitting room with

a desk and two chairs and a hat stand. A second door sits
ajar, revealing a bedroom on the other side.

I stand in the center of the room, looking around uncertainly. Georg has cleaned in preparation for my arrival,
I can tell, and opened the windows to try without success
to clear some of the mustiness from the dank gray space.

He coughs once, then a second time stronger. "Are you
unwell?" I ask.

"Not at all. I've had this blasted cold ever since I came
back from sea."

"Have you seen a doctor? Papa has a physician in the city
on rue de la Rochelle."

He shakes his head. "There's no time. It's just a cold."
He gestures to the cardboard box I carry. "What's that?"

I open it, revealing the small cake that I had picked up
for him on impulse before leaving Paris, yellow with just
a touch of whipped cream on the top. "Happy Birthday,"
I say.

Several expressions cross his face at once—uncertainty,
then bewilderment and finally joy. "I cannot remember
when someone last celebrated my birthday."

"Would you like some?"

"No, thank you."

I set down the box, feeling foolish.

"Not just this moment," he amends. "I need to leave you
for a short while to confer with one of my colleagues," he
apologizes. "But if you wouldn't mind working on without me, perhaps we could have some cake when I return."

"Of course." In fact, I am uneasy at the notion of staying here alone in the desolate hotel room. I consider asking

if I might take the documents with me to our apartment, then decide against it.

"I'll be back as soon as I can."

Watching him leave, a strange sense of longing floods through me. It's the room, I tell myself, the fact that I don't want to be alone here. The space feels even colder and darker without him.

My eyes drift to the pile of binders and notes over by the desk, the ones that Georg has not given to me. Now would be the perfect time to search for the information Ignatz has insisted that I procure. But I cannot. It is not just that I am nervous, uncertain when Georg will return. There is something in the way he looks at me, filled with such trust. I don't want to betray that.

Tea, I decide. I peer into the bedroom. Unlike the sitting area, it has not been tidied for my benefit and the feeling of Georg is everywhere, in the still slightly tousled sheets, the smell of his aftershave, which lingers in the still-wet brush by the basin. Searching for tea, I open the cupboard, which is well stocked with crackers and dried fruit. Georg does not, I surmise, like to stop working and leave the hotel to eat.

I set the kettle, then walk to the basin, peering into the egg-shaped cracked mirror above it. Georg stands here each morning, washing and getting dressed. Does he ever think of me?

Alarmed by the thought, I step away from the mirror and closer to his bed. I run my hand over the pillowcase, imagining him there, asleep. This is silliness, a schoolgirl's crush. But I'm twenty years old, and I have a fiancé waiting for me.

A sharp whistling jars me from my thoughts and I leap back. The kettle. I pour the tea with shaking hands, then hurry back to the front room.

I thumb through the pile of memos, sorting before starting on one about the German battleship fleet. The language is complex and I frequently turn to the dictionary, but I soon become engrossed and the translation flows more smoothly.

The door opens and Georg walks in. I look up, surprised at the time that has passed and the fact that it is nearly ten o'clock.

"How's your progress?"

"Good, I think." In truth, it is easier to work without Georg and the temptation to talk. I push the notes toward him, smelling as I do the faintly sour odor of wine on his breath.

He stands behind me and reaches down. "This passage here." Georg gestures as if to demonstrate his point, and I find myself staring as his hands—the long tapered fingers, soft nail beds almost improbably well-manicured. He bends closer, his warmth against my back.

Then he straightens. "Shall we have some cake?" Not waiting for an answer, he cuts two pieces and passes one to me. He drops to the seat across from mine and takes a bite. "Delicious. Thank you."

I set my plate aside and finish augmenting the translation to include the paragraph he indicated, then pass it to him. He leans over to read it. There is a space between his collar and hair where the skin is exposed, and I am seized with the urge to put my lips there. What is wrong with me?

I clear my throat. "Let me know once you've had the chance to review these if you have any questions."

"I shall." But his eyes glaze over the notes, seeming not to see them. He yawns and sets down his plate. "You said you had an errand in Paris. Where did you go?"

The question is perhaps intrusive, but I do not mind. "To a dressmaker," I say. "I had a...fitting."

"Not for one of those formal dresses, I hope. After all of the makeup and ruffles the women wear around here, you are positively refreshing."

"Thank you." I shift uneasily.

He stands again, walking to the mantelpiece and picking up a framed photograph of a ship, a row of men lined up neatly on the gangplank. "Your men?" I ask.

"They were. It all fell apart at the end." His words run together now, slurred slightly by drink. "We received orders to move north and engage the British navy there. We knew it was futile—the war was all but over and we were defeated. But we commanded the men to proceed. They refused. They were starving and demoralized. They didn't want to die, too. It was madness, Margot." The full sorrow of the sentence crashes down on my name. "Sailors fighting sailors. Two of my own men killed one another.

"The war cost me everything," Georg adds abruptly, setting the photo back down unsteadily. He is open and exposed in a way that I have not yet seen.

"Your brother..."

He nods. "I lost my father when I was on the ship, too.

I received word that he was dying but it was a matter of hours and we were at sea. There was nothing that could be done. It was just days after Peter died at Jutland so he never even knew, which I think was in itself a blessing."

He continues, "I was studying at university when the war broke out." His eyes have a faraway look and his voice sounds like mine when I speak of travel. I see him them as a boy, wide-eyed and bright with a future in front of him. He is so broken now, like so many others. I am seized by the urge to take him into my arms. Can he be healed or is he too far gone?

"You can still go back."

He smiles, as though talking to an indulgent child. "That's kind of you to say. But what school would have me? I'm twenty-five, no, twenty-six." He gestures toward the rest of the cake, which sits uneaten on the table. "My hands shake like an old man's and I can't concentrate. That was a younger man's dream." He leans back resigned. "But if we can get this right, that is, if we can come up with an order of things that makes sense, that would mean it was all for something. It has to have meant something, doesn't it?" He searches my eyes and there is a kind of desperation in his voice.

Our conversation is intimate now, as though we have known each other years and not just days. "The war took so many good men," he adds. "I suppose that is why you are on your own?"

I swallow, uncomfortable at his abrupt shift in focus to me. "There was someone."

"You were engaged?"

I nod. "My fiancé was at the Marne."

"A tragedy. So you understand, then, what it was like with my brother." I realize, too late, that he has come away with the impression that my fiancé died. There was a time when I thought that Stefan was dead. Papa had come back to our rooms at college at midday when I knew he should have been holding supervisions. A telegram was clutched in his hand and his face was the strangest shade of gray. "Darling," he said. We'd both taken to speaking more English while here, part of our futile quest to fit in, and it spilled over to the times when we were alone. "It's Stefan…he's missing."

"Soldiers go missing all of the time," I said, my voice wavering at the end, me comforting Papa when it should have been the reverse.

He shook his head, and I took the paper from his out-stretched fingers to spare him from having to tell me the rest. Words leaped from the page piecemeal, rising up and forming a tapestry of images in my mind. A bomb had blown a crater a quarter of a mile wide, decimating the trench he'd been in. Stefan and his whole unit were gone, and the severity of the attack had left no hope of survivors.

Stefan was dead. I had imagined it secretly in the places so dark I could scarcely acknowledge them. Had I brought it on him? Even through my sadness, I knew that such things were not possible, that the universe did not operate according to the whims of my mind.

In the days that followed, my sadness mixed with new ideas. I could remain in England and take classes, or perhaps travel farther abroad as a governess. Surely in my grief and my search for a new direction, I'd be allowed more than the usual latitude.

Word that Stefan was alive did not come for nearly six weeks. "Found in a hospital in Belgium. But, darling, he's been quite badly wounded. His legs have been hurt, there may possibly be other injuries, as well. You must prepare yourself."

I was silent for several minutes, overwhelmed by a combination of shock and relief and, to my shame, a tinge of disappointment. "Will he make it?"

"I believe so. He's very strong of will, according to Walter." My uncle had been using his contacts at the ministry to procure information. "It must be the thought of coming back to you that kept him alive."

"That's wonderful news." But my voice was flat and without meaning. I had come to accept Stefan's death in recent weeks. I'd been sad for him, of course. But freed from the expectations of marrying him, I'd begun to make plans. Now he was back and the visions of a life for myself crumbled to dust and blew away with the breeze, as if they'd never been there at all. The old world began to tighten around me like a noose.

"Do you believe in God?" Georg asks, drawing me from my memories. I tilt my head at the sudden shift in conversation.His tone is philosophical now. "You're a Jewess, aren't you?"

"Yes." His words strike me as somehow abrupt, just short of rude.

"Are you religious?"

"I suppose." Mine is the naive and childlike sort of be-

lief that comes from things taught rather than deeply considered. Religion isn't something I ever questioned; it was
just something that we did, part of the expectation of who
I was to be. But it was not something I thought about on
a deeper level. "You?"

"I stopped believing, really, the day I saw my brother
swallowed into the sea." He is asking whether my faith was
shaken, as well, by losing someone I loved.

"The men were awful to the Jewish sailors, I'm afraid,"
Georg says. "They hazed them, beat them, took their food.
Once there was a particularly grievous assault of an, ahem,
sexual nature." He is clearly uncomfortable but unwilling
to shield me from the truth.

"Oh!" Stefan's letters had given no hint. There had been
only cheer in his writing, bright talk of the future we would
have, building a house. It was as if he had to doggedly persist in his belief that he would return unscathed—a belief
that was shattered nevertheless at the Marne.

My guilt rises. After all Stefan has been through, he de-
serves a life full of joy, a hero's welcome or at least a woman
who wants to be by his side.

"It was a horrible thing, the way they treated the Jewish
lads," Georg says. "That's why Palestine is so important."

"Oh?" I flare. "You want to ship all the Jews off to the
desert?"

"No, of course not. But a home of their own, a safe
haven."

"Germany is our home," I persist. My family came to
Prussia in the seventeenth century, when only a few Jews
were allowed in, and stayed, our lives interwoven with the

fabric of the non-Jewish Germans who were our neighbors and friends. I cannot identify with some strange Semitic land I've never seen.

Georg sits, staring wordlessly over my shoulder. "And you?" I find myself emboldened to ask, pushed by the need to change the subject. "Do you have a fiancée?" He shakes his head. "I've never been involved with a woman," he confesses. "I noticed them, of course, like any young man would, but there was work and my studies. And they always seemed interested in the most superficial things. I've never found one I could speak to as I do you." This last comment, too intimate for the short time we have known each other, catches me off guard. Yet I feel exactly the same.

"I thought there would be time. And then well, war changes a person. Have you ever been to a carnival, one of those with the merry-go-round that spins so very fast that afterward when you lie in bed at night you feel like you are still spinning?" I nod, trying to follow the story without letting images of Georg in bed intrude. "I lay awake at night and I hear the cannon fire against the ship and the screams of the men around us as they sank to a cold watery death while we stood hopelessly by."

He buries his head in his hands and I start toward him, seized by the urge to comfort him with more than just words, to wrap him in my arms and rock him like a child. But as I near he stands and takes a step back. "And that is why I will never marry or be of any good to any woman." His eyes are steely, as though he regrets having let down his guard and confided in me. "Good evening, Margot."

He gets up and walks into the bedroom. I stare at the now-closed door, stunned.

I take my coat and start for the hallway. "Margot, wait…" I turn back as the bedroom door opens again. I wait for him to apologize for his outburst. "We won't be able to work tomorrow," he says instead. I wonder if I have done something wrong, whether my work is not pleasing to him. "The dinner party," he explains. I recall the gathering in Paris that both he and Papa are dreading.

"Of course. If you'd like, I can keep working on my own."

"It's not that. Rather, I was wondering…" He is gazing at me squarely now. "Would you like to accompany me?" It takes me several seconds to comprehend he is asking me to go as his date. "Perhaps if I ask your father…"

"No!" I say, too vehemently. Papa will never approve and then he will tell Georg the truth about Stefan. "That is, I told Papa I would go with him." It is a lie. "I will meet you there." Better, too, to avoid the many questions from Papa that Georg's invitation would provoke.

I walk from the hotel hurriedly. The feelings Georg stirs in me are unlike any I have ever known. But until now, at least I could take comfort in the fact that they were one-sided, a pretense that has been shattered by his invitation. How is it possible that someone as attractive and worldly as Georg could be interested in me?

A few minutes later, I barrel into the flat. "I should like to join you for the dinner party, if you don't mind," I say before Papa can look up. Papa does not respond, but his eyebrows lift. For so long I have tried to avoid the social obligations of the conference.

"I hadn't thought you would want to." He had mentioned the dinner party previously only to ask my forbearance in missing our usual Sabbath meal together, not with any serious thought that I would want to go.

"I'd enjoy an evening in the city."

"I'd love you to join me." He smiles at the prospect of my escorting him. Celia's lack of any official status and the quiet nature of their relationship makes it impossible for her to attend such functions with him and so he often goes alone. Then a light dawns in his eyes, as if he suddenly understands my newfound interest in the occasion. His brow furrows with consternation. "Margot, *liebchen*. About Captain Richwalder…"

"I'm helping him with the translation, that's all. It's good for my language skills." He dips his chin in that way that signals he isn't convinced by what I've said. "You don't like him," I observe, trying to hide my disappointment.

"He fights for a living. He must be at least ten years older than you."

"Five only," I counter. *Technically six.*

"And he's odd," Papa continues, undeterred.

"It's the combat, Papa, that's all. The things that he saw and he heard…" I stop, realizing that my words are revealing the extent of our conversation, an intimacy that goes well beyond just work.

"That may be the case," he concedes. "The war changed people in so many ways and we all have to live with who we are now. But Georg's not Jewish." Finally, we are getting to the heart of the issue. Why, I wonder, thinking of Krysia and Marcin, should that matter? We have become so assimilated. Papa doesn't even wear a yarmulke anymore. There are some things, though, that are still sacrosanct. Intermarriage would mean children that might not be raised Jewish. But I cannot engage in this debate with Papa without admitting to him that there is something to his question.

"Of course not," I say quickly, avoiding the confrontation any other answer would bring. I swallow over the lump that has formed in my throat. "Anyway, I'm engaged to Stefan." The explanation hangs hollowly and without conviction.

His brow wrinkles. "Maybe we should get away for a bit when the conference is over." He fears that he has been neglecting me and that I've gravitated toward Georg out of loneliness. "Perhaps this summer we should rent a villa on the coast." Does he expect us to be here that long?

Not waiting for a response, he turns back to his papers, our conversation apparently over. I walk uneasily toward my room, then stop, turning back. There is no one in the world to whom I feel closer than Papa. Yet despite our deep affection, there are vast areas of darkness, things unsaid, parts of ourselves that we cannot share. Once upon a time the idea of keeping secrets from Papa was unfathomable. There was the unspoken between us—the fact that he and Celia were together—but that was not quite a lie. Our trust is a thread that, once pulled at, is swiftly unraveling.

Later that night I lay awake thinking about Georg. Why hadn't I told him the truth about Stefan, the fact that he is still alive and waiting for me back home? It would have been

the natural response, but now it is too late. Georg is a man
of principle and ethics. I feared that if he knew I am not by
Stefan's side, he would judge me less than honorable. But
it is not his judgment I am feeling—it is my own shame.

I remember Georg, standing too close behind me.
Warmth rises from my legs and I bring my hand low, trying to silence the feeling, but this only increases my longing
for him. I have no business thinking such things. I know
so little of matters between men and women. With Stefan
there had been a few innocent gropes. I've heard whispers
of the other girls at school and learned a bit from novels, the
ones I did not let Papa see. But the rest is a gaping hole in
my comprehension, a curtain I cannot pull back. My secret
thoughts have always been nameless and faceless until now.
I press harder and my desire crests, then ebbs. Finally, I turn
and close my eyes, still seeing Georg's face in my mind.

7

"Are you ready?" Papa stands at the door to my room, waiting patiently.

"Just another minute, please." As he retreats, I pull back a lock of hair for what feels like the hundredth time, but it breaks free once more. I throw down the pin, frustrated. I have never been any good at dressing and polishing and I always wind up looking as unkempt as before I started. It seems a waste trying. "The lack of a mother's touch," I heard Tante Celia remark once when she thought I wasn't listening. She tries to help in her own clumsy way, buying me lipstick and powder for my nose, but they reflect her own taste, stiff and heavily scented. I imagine my mother here, smoothing my hair, giving some advice on what I should and should not say at dinner. A rare and unexpected wave of longing for her shoots through me.

I take a final glance in the mirror, patting with resignation the tangle of curls that have ceded into a tight ball from the dampness and fog. My eyes peer out, too large for my face, making me appear something of an owl.

An hour later, we arrive at the Swiss ambassador's residence, a Le Marais town house double the usual width with carved wrought-iron balconies. The drawing room where drinks are being served is a staid affair, with plain beige drapes and a hardwood floor that shows its scuffs through the polish. In contrast to the wild galas I've attended previously, the mood is quiet, even somber. The German delegates cluster on the opposite side of the room from their hosts, like adolescent boys and girls at a dance back home, too shy to mingle.

As Papa hands our coats to the butler, I scan the room but do not see Georg. Perhaps, since I'd declined his invitation to come as his guest, he has decided to defy expectations and remain at the hotel working. I am seized with the urge to flee back to Versailles and do the same.

A moment later I sense him, lifting my head as his square frame fills the doorway that separates the foyer from the great room. It is the first time I have ever seen him in his dress uniform, resplendent with the rich blue fabric that contours to the gold-braided shoulders. Medals of valor adorn the broad expanse of his chest. Suddenly it is as if the air has been sucked from the room, making it impossible to breathe.

All female eyes turn toward him. A handsome man, even an enemy soldier, is an oasis in the desert that was left behind by those who went to the front and never returned or who came home broken like Stefan. The room shrinks around Georg as he surveys the room, his expression grim. He was late intentionally, I decide, wanting to spend as little time here as possible. His steely eyes take in the gathering. There is a seriousness to him, a wisdom and worldliness beyond his years. The things he has seen have worn grooves in him, like driftwood pounded by the water, making him fascinating in a way that other men simply are not.

His head turns then in my direction and as our eyes meet, a light dawns within him. I hold his gaze, mindful that I am staring but unable to look away. His face breaks wide open then with the vulnerability of a young child. The people and sound fade, leaving just Georg and me and then endless space between us. In that moment, the walls crumble, revealing the attraction that should not exist, but nonetheless does.

Papa is at my side now, but my ears buzz with such a din that I cannot hear what he is saying. I pretend to listen, still watching Georg out of the corner of my eye as he crosses the room. I am filled with shame at the way my pulse quickens. But the daughter of a British viscount whom I've encountered at a few social functions intercepts Georg and takes his arm. She leads him to the fireplace, a ravenous dog about to devour a steak dinner. My heart sinks. Leigh Arrington is an alabaster beauty, with a tall, willowy grace I could never hope to match. I feel silly and childlike by comparison. How I wish we were back in the drafty study at the hotel, just the two of us.

Georg shifts slightly and his expression is pained. His eyes meet mine over her head and the look of longing is unmistakable. He would rather be alone with me, as well, I realize, suppressing a flutter.

The sound of a piano, its cadence familiar, blossoms from the corner of the room. I turn, delighted to see Krysia seated at the keyboard. I had not known she would be playing tonight. The sound is more fulsome than usual, Marcin at his cello beside her. I start toward Krysia, but a tuxedoed man I do not recognize reaches the piano first. He pages through the sheet music over her shoulder and I expect her to be annoyed, but she does not appear so. A moment later, the man whispers something, then walks away. Krysia begins playing a Chopin piece, presumably the one the man requested.

As the last note fades to a smattering of polite applause, I approach. "You didn't mention you would be here tonight."

"You didn't ask."

"I've never heard you two play together. You sound wonderful."

"Marcin is the real artist," she remarks. He smiles but does not look up from tuning his instrument. "I'm going to take a break, my dear," she tells him. She steps away from the piano as he begins to play a solo, her eyes wide with adoration. Krysia always seems so strong; it is strange to watch her step back and let Marcin take center stage. But she is right, there is a poetry to the way his fingers move over the strings, a fluidity to his bowing that even a neophyte such as myself can recognize as world-class.

"I'm glad you're here," Krysia says. "There's something I need to... Good evening." She switches topics abruptly, glancing over my shoulder. I turn and find Georg standing behind me, too close.

"Captain Richwalder." There is a note of playfulness to my formality. He does not answer, but stares at me. It is the gown, one that Celia had picked out for me. The pink material clings long and lean to my torso and the neckline is much more daring than the everyday blouses I wear to work for him. My mother's drop pearl necklace circles my throat.

"Margot." He recovers, then leans forward and kisses me on the cheek, the scent of his aftershave reminiscent of his rooms, only more intense. I freeze—though not improper, it is hardly the traditional kiss on the hand. His lips are warm and fleeting on my cheek, high and close to my ear. He pauses, breath lingering in my hair, and I fight the urge to move even closer. As he straightens, his expression is confused, as though he had not himself quite planned to behave in such a manner.

Beside me, Krysia clears her throat. "Please excuse me," I say. "Georg, this is Krysia Smok."

"A pleasure," she says, but her voice is devoid of its usual warmth and her hand remains at her side.

"Krysia is Polish," I offer, trying to break the ice that has formed suddenly.

"From Krakow to be exact."

He grimaces. "Southern Poland is a hotbed for communists. The traitor Rosa Luxemburg for one." His voice is harsher than usual.

Krysia stiffens at his reference to the recently killed activist. "Rosa and I were classmates in school. She was shot like a dog, her body dumped in a canal. Is this the world we've come to?"

"I certainly don't condone such violence. But the communists are a great menace to our society back home. Law and order is needed," he adds firmly.

"But in a democracy, the ideals of different groups—"

"All have their place in an orderly forum." I understand now why Krysia and he instantly dislike each other.

Krysia looks away, unable to continue the debate calmly and unwilling to rise to the bait. "Krakow is beautiful," she says, returning to more neutral waters. "The City of Kings, we call it. Castles and churches and the mountains close by. You should try to see it someday."

Georg shakes his head. "It's landlocked. I'm afraid my love pulls me toward the sea."

"'One may find beauty where one least expects it,'" Krysia prods. "'There are more things in heaven and earth...'"

"'...than are dreamt of in your philosophy,'" he finishes for her. There is an awkward silence between them. Georg's expression is uncomfortable, Krysia's icy. "Margot, I need to speak with your father about some matters. If you'll excuse me." Without waiting for a response, he walks across the room, leaving me deflated by his departure, as well as the realization that the two people I've met and like best since coming to Paris do not seem to at all like each other.

"So that's your German," she says, a note of disdain to her voice.

"He's not 'my' German," I correct, annoyed. "He's German—as am I. What was that last bit about?"

"It's from Shakespeare's *Hamlet*. It means that one should not profess to know all of the answers—and that the world holds a great many mysteries and wonders for one to see." Her bottom lip curls. "Not that he would understand."

"Krysia, you've hardly met him."

"He's a fascist soldier and—forgive me—a German."

"It is a hard thing to be rejected for who you are," I say, throwing back at her the words she'd used to describe the pain of being shunned by Marcin's Jewish family.

"Perhaps." But I can tell from the way her jaw is set that she will never accept him.

Over Krysia's shoulder, I watch Georg and Papa together,

heads bowed low in quiet conversation. The two could not be more different—the scholar and the warrior—yet I love them both so much. *Love.* I stop, caught off guard by my thought. It is the first time I have ever allowed myself to think of Georg that way and now it has leaped out and I cannot stop it—like trying to put paste back into a tube. Is such a thing possible after just a few days? My feelings for Georg are undeniably real, but at the same time they change nothing—not the fact that I cannot be with him, or that Stefan is still waiting for me.

"He should be thanking God for the Bolsheviks," Krysia mutters under her breath.

I turn to her, grateful for the reprieve from my thoughts. "How can you say that?"

"Because the red menace, as they call it, is the only thing that's keeping the Big Four from destroying Germany entirely. They need your country strong enough that communism cannot spread across Europe like wildfire, but not so strong that it can cause trouble again. If it weren't for Russia, the Western powers would send Germany back into the nineteenth century. Of course, he would not understand that." Before I can respond, Krysia returns to the piano and joins Marcin as he plays.

Standing alone, I scan the room for Papa and Georg. Across the party, one of the servers, older and more portly than the others, catches my eye. I gasp. Ignatz. He makes his way over to fill my wineglass. "What are you doing here?"

"Working. My cousin is a catering manager and I fill in sometimes for a bit of cash."

"Oh," I reply flatly, unplaced by his answer. There are

dozens of parties in Paris each week—it makes no sense that he happens to be at this one.

"And I wanted to see you," he continues, getting to the heart of the matter. My stomach sinks. "Have you gotten the documents for me?"

"You only asked me yesterday. There's hardly been time." I study his face wondering if he believes me. Could he possibly have known that Georg had left me alone in his rooms the previous night with full access to his files?

He does not press the point, instead gesturing across the room with his head. "That's him over there, isn't it?"

His question is not in earnest. The only military man in the room, Georg would be hard to miss. "Perhaps I shall speak with him myself." Ignatz's tone is menacing. "Or maybe your father…"

"No!" I yelp, more loudly than I intended. A woman standing behind me turns to look over her shoulder. Ignatz could reveal everything before all of these people and destroy Papa.

"Don't play games with us, Margot," he says, his voice low with menace. "Time is of the essence and…"

"Darling," Papa says, coming to my side, "is something wrong?"

"Not at all," I say, searching for an explanation for my extended conversation with a server. But when I turn around, Ignatz has disappeared. "I'm going to freshen up before we are seated." I make my way from the reception, then double back around to the piano. "He's here," I whisper to Krysia from behind.

She does not stop playing. "I know. That is what I was

trying to tell you. It is just like that fool. Remain calm and I will see what I can learn."

A bell rings on the far side of the room, signaling dinner. At the door to the dining room I meet Georg, who is standing to one side, trying without success to adjust his tie. "May I?" I offer. It is something I have done as long as I can remember with Papa, smoothing out the knot, tucking the corners just so.

His face relaxes. "Please."

I struggle to keep my fingers from trembling against his skin, the lump in his throat moves slightly beneath my touch. "There. Much better."

"Thank you." He coughs once, then again. "How are you enjoying the party?"

Our eyes meet and we laugh, understanding just how much we both hate being here. Then his expression turns serious. "It's good, I suppose, to be out. I'm sorry if I offended your friend the pianist with my political talk. Spending so much time at sea has robbed me of all sense of polite conversation."

"Not at all."

"There you are." Papa comes up behind us.

"I've taken the liberty of arranging to be seated near you," Georg says. My breath catches. "There are some matters related to the Ruhr proposal that I'd like to discuss." He was talking, of course, to Papa, not me. But when we reach the table the placards indicate that the seating is the customary man-woman-man insofar as the lopsided numbers permit, and I am nevertheless sandwiched in between Georg and my father. Seeing the arrangement, a frown flickers across Papa's face.

The table is set plainly, I notice as I sit down in the chair that Georg has pulled back. The cloth napkins are crude, the knives and forks just a step above everyday kitchen silver. But this is more than just the lingering austerity of the war. Rather, the message from our hosts is clear—we will sit down with you Germans because we must, but we will never accept you as equals.

As the first course, salmon croquette, is served, Georg engages in conversation with a Swiss military attaché across the table. "If we can make them see that the German navy can help maintain peace and stability in the new order," he begins doggedly. It is not the first time I have heard him express his views, and there is an optimism and hope in his voice that lightens my heart. But the faces across the table are skeptical.

"Surely you are aware of Weber's writings on the subject of the military-economic nexus in Germany?" a Dutchman at the far end of the table asks. Georg falters. Though he speaks well about matters in which he has experience, he is self-conscious about having not completed his education.

"Will there still be a Germany?" I blurt out, trying to help him by changing the subject. All eyes around us turn in my direction.

"Pardon me?" a startled older woman to Papa's right asks.

I clear my throat, too far gone to turn back. "It's just that the country is so young." Though Germany has been unified for all of my life, it is easy to forget that just half a century ago, when Papa was a boy, it was a series of fragmented states. Prussia, Bavaria and the other regions are still in many ways more distinct that homogenous. "The strain of the treaty, if it doesn't go well, may be more than the republic can bear."

"How can you speak of such things about your own country?" Leigh Arrington asks.

"Our remaining silent will not make the issue disappear. We must meet the question head-on."

"My dear, is it your place to trouble with such things?" The question, from a monocled man I do not recognize, is condescending.

"I, for one, am most interested in what Fraulein Rosenthal has to say," Georg declares, coming to my defense. Out of the corner of my eye, I see Papa nod slightly with approval. His reservations notwithstanding, Papa is pleased that Georg respects my views and treats me as an intellectual equal.

The main course, mutton in too-rich gravy, is served. The conversation turns elsewhere to a debate about North Africa about which I have no knowledge or views. Beneath the table, Georg's fingers skim the back of my hand. I wonder if it is an accident, but then his fingers close firmly around mine. I can feel his eyes on me, trying to catch my gaze to ask if I mind. But I am unable to look up. Papa continues speaking to Georg above my head, noticing nothing.

With my free hand, I sample a piece of baguette, savoring the buttery flavor. Passover had ended just a few weeks ago and it had been nearly torture to walk past the patisseries only to face the dry, sawdustlike matzo Papa had procured from the city's only functioning Jewish bakery. As I reach for my water glass, there is a clattering across the room, a silver tray falling from a server's hands and crashing to the floor. Startled, Georg jumps up and reaches instinctively for the pistol he no longer carries.

"Never mind," I soothe, putting my arm on his and willing him to sit down again. But he is shaken, a gray pallor to his complexion. Though he is not outwardly wounded like Stefan, Georg is broken in quieter ways. There are other signs, as well—he eats quickly, as though food might be taken from him, drinks each mouthful of water as if it might be his last. "Perhaps we should get some air," I suggest.

"This room is infernally warm," he agrees. "I've heard there are some lovely gardens. Do you think we might take a stroll?"

I hesitate, glancing at Papa, who is ensconced in a conversation with a man on his far side. "I'm going to powder my nose," I say, gesturing slightly with my head toward the door, prompting him to meet me.

A moment later, I slip into the garden where Georg waits in the shadows. Outside the spring air is cool, but not unpleasantly so, the smell of fresh honeysuckle coming from the side of the path. A fountain trickles unseen in the darkness.

"This is much better." He chuckles as we walk down the path, the voices inside fading. I hope he might offer me his arm, but he does not. "I thought that woman, LeeAnn…"

"Leigh Arrington," I correct, secretly pleased he does not remember her name.

"Yes, that's the one. I thought she might faint when you offered up your views."

"I never should have said anything."

"Nonsense. You spoke your mind forthrightly and well

and the conversation was better for it. You were only voicing what the others were thinking but were too cowardly to say. I admire your courage."

Courage. If only he knew. "I hold my tongue as often as I can. Women where I come from aren't encouraged to speak or do much, you see. We're meant to go to the parties and salons, to look nice and act pleasant." I comprehend fully for the first time the truth of my words. Even Papa, who encouraged me to read and learn, did so just for the sake of knowledge—but what good was it all if I didn't use it? "That's why I enjoy our work…" I falter.

His lips twitch with amusement. "I'm glad to provide a diversion."

"That's not what I meant at all." What I do, with him and for him, means so much more. But I cannot find the words. "It's just so frustrating, watching the hypocrisy day after day. Wilson came with promises of freedom and self-determination, the very premise on which America was founded. But the reality seems to only be freedom for some."

"Yes, but if we give everyone those rights, it will be anarchy. And right now, when we are among the defeated and seeking our own rights, we must be most careful."

I stop and turn to him. "No, it is exactly now, when we are fighting for our own rights, that we must stand in solidarity with others who seek theirs."

Georg is silent for a moment. "Of course. Sometimes, amid all of the political struggles, I forget why we are here in the first place. You are like true north on a compass, Margot, and you help me find the way back." The statement, too bold and naked for the short time we have known each other, hangs awkwardly between us.

"It's been a beautiful spring," I offer, eager to break the tension.

"Yes, though I understand the farmers are quite mad to have some rain." I nod. They've only just been able to return to tilling the fields after years of battle. It is difficult to fathom the disaster a drought might bring to a country just coming back from the edge of starvation.

A breeze blows through the garden then, pulling a piece of my hair from its moorings. Georg reaches out and brushes the lock from my face, then stops, hand suspended midair. It is my scar, illuminated in the moonlight, that has drawn his attention. A small colorless indentation just below my left ear, it appeared suddenly years earlier after the flu had passed, a reaction perhaps to the medicines that they tried. It is normally not visible, but tonight with my hair pulled higher, he can see it for the first time.

I hold my breath, wondering if he will find it distasteful. But he continues to stare at me longingly, eyes wide. "Margot..." He fumbles to find further words but cannot.

We continue walking in silence. Though we work beside each other each day, the air between us is somehow different here. "I'm glad you decided to attend the dinner tonight," he says, then coughs slightly. "I mean, even if it isn't with me."

I touch his forearm. "Georg, about that. It was just easier to come with Papa."

"I understand. He wouldn't approve." He believes my refusal was about him, that he somehow wasn't good enough.

I want to tell him that wasn't it at all, but how can I without explaining the truth about my engagement to Stefan?

"Your father doesn't like me." It is not a question.

"That's not true," I protest quickly. I touch his forearm. "He thinks you are incredibly smart." I stop and pull back, a blush creeping into my cheeks. Now Georg knows that we have been talking about him. "It's only that he is a pacifist. He was against the war."

"None of us wanted the war," he replies. "That is, none of the real people. There are old men, of course, in Berlin and Paris and London using the military for their own ends."

"You talk like it is a chess game."

"In a sense, it is."

"And you don't mind being a pawn?"

"If wars are to be fought, they should be led by men who can do it well. Fewer lives are lost that way. A well-waged battle can bring war to a quicker end." I do not answer. Through the window, I see Papa talking to one of the other guests.

"You're quite fond of him," Georg observed. Fireflies flicker in the distance, then disappear into the blackness like shooting stars.

"It's always just been the two of us."

"He's a good man." He turns away to stifle a cough. "Though I fear academia is an ill fit with the cut and thrust of politics. As poor of a fit as time at battle." They are both outsiders here. "You must warn him to be careful. I should not want to see him get hurt." His pupils have grown large in the moonlight, two wide circles swimming in pools of gray.

Thinking of the information I shared with Ignatz and the danger I've brought to Papa, my consternation rises. "You make it sound like war, not a peace conference." Another sharp breeze cuts across the garden then and I shiver involuntarily. Before I can protest, Georg unbuttons his coat and with a swift motion brings it around my shoulders as he had the night we first met. His scent, wool and fresh soap, wafts up around me, and in that moment it is as if he is holding me in his embrace. "Thank you."

"Your necklace is beautiful. May I?" I nod and he brings his finger to my throat, skin warm against mine. The back of his nail grazes my skin as he lifts the gem.

"It was my mother's." Papa had given it to me as a sweet-sixteen present, pulled from the box at the bank that still holds my mother's better pieces, the ones he considers me too impetuous and careless yet to wear.

He lets the gem fall gently back to my throat, and as he pulls away his hand trembles. He's scared, I realize. Georg has always been an island, too remote to let anything touch him. Until now. Am I the same? Though I have been involved with Stefan, these feelings are terrifying.

The back door to the house opens and a silhouette appears. "Margot, are you out there?"

"Coming, Papa."

"I can escort you home," Georg offers in a low voice as we walk back across the garden. "That way your father will not have to interrupt his conversation. Perhaps the driver could take us down the Champs-Élysée to see the lights." A shift from the man who had said a few days earlier that he was not in Paris to play tourist.

Georg's jacket, I remember as we step into the light of the house, which now feels garish. I slip it from my shoulders and try to hand it to him, but it is too late—Papa has already seen. Confusion, then realization and concern, cross his face in an instant.

Inside, the party has broken up at the table, the men retreating to the library for brandy and cigars. "Papa, Georg has offered to take me home." I no longer pretend to call him by his formal title.

"That is, if you'd like me to escort Margot back to the hotel." Georg steps in to save me from having to ask. A fine layer of perspiration coats his upper lip.

I watch Papa struggle inwardly, his own desire to remain in Paris and see Celia colliding with his wanting to keep me and Georg apart. "You'll take her straight back?" Georg towers over Papa, a giant. But it is Papa who seems somehow larger now, fierce in his protectiveness of me.

"It's just a ride, Papa," I nudge gently. "Georg is hardly a stranger." Something flickers across Georg's face. To him it is something more. A ride back to Versailles, just the two of us, a goodbye on the steps of our building....

"Fine," Papa relents.

Georg coughs once, then a second time harder. "I'll get your coat."

As Georg disappears, I spy Krysia in a vestibule, motioning for me to join her. "I didn't have time to speak with you before with everyone around. I've done some checking, and I'm afraid Ignatz is for real. I should have guessed it. He isn't very subtle. He spends money far beyond what he could earn serving drinks and cakes to a bunch of starving artists. He's gotten in with some folks with legitimate connections. And he's not going to leave you alone, I'm afraid. His taking the risk to come here tonight is proof positive of that. He must consider you a terribly valuable asset. Any step out of line and your father will be revealed as the leak."

Papa's career, I lament, ruined because of my own stupidity. Anger rises up in me, then a sense of futility. Krysia had been encouraging me to be my own person. Instead, I've become a chess piece in the very way I'd criticized Georg of being. But if I don't help, I will discredit Papa. "I hate politics."

"It's always politics, isn't it, unless it is our own point of view? Then it is the truth."

A sharp coughing erupts across the room. Georg. He has stepped from the cloakroom and gasps for air, his face turning red. Suddenly he slumps against the wall and his eyes roll back. He collapses to the floor.

"Georg!" I start forward, but Krysia puts her arm on mine. "Herr Mitten is a doctor. Let him take care of this." A group of men swarm Georg, tending to him, loosening his collar. Let him be all right, I pray. Minutes pass with agonizing slowness. Outside comes the shrill cry of an ambulance siren.

I step forward again, desperate to be with Georg. He needs me.

But Papa is beside me now, holding me back as medics put Georg on a stretcher and carry him from the house. I turn to him frantically. "We should go to the hospital."

"It isn't our place. The other delegation members will look after him."

I press against his grasp. "But…"

"We should go."

I start to protest. The notion of returning to Versailles without knowing if Georg is safe is unfathomable.

"I will check," Krysia whispers. Papa herds me toward the car, the siren wailing long and desolate as the ambulance bearing Georg disappears into the night.

8

The next morning I've just finished steeping my tea when the bell rings, signaling an unexpected visitor below. Hearing footsteps on the stairway, I wonder if I should wake Papa in case it is official business. But when I open the door to the flat, Krysia appears on the landing. I am surprised; she has not come to Versailles at all in the months since we moved out here, much less unannounced.

"Did I wake you?" I shake my head. Worried about Georg, I'd slept little all night. I look over my shoulder. The apartment is a mess—Papa's discarded notes are strewn across the floor in crumpled balls, and dirty glasses and filled ashtrays litter the tables. Picturing Krysia's elegant flat, I step in front of the doorway, trying to block her view.

"I'm sorry not to have called first," she says, appearing too large in the narrow, crooked corridor. "But I had to catch an early train and I didn't want to wake anyone."

"Not at all. I believe arriving unexpectedly is a tradition I started."

She smiles slightly, but her expression is forced. Has she come in person to bring me bad news? "What is it? Is it Georg?"

"Everything is fine," she replies hurriedly.

"Won't you come in? I've just made tea."

"No, thank you. I have an errand out of the city so I won't be able to stay long. Perhaps we could walk instead? It really is a lovely morning."

Outside the air is unseasonably warm but not unpleasant, with a gentle breeze wafting lavender from the fields to the east, clearing the smells of the street.

"He has pneumonia," says Krysia a moment later.

My shoulders slump with relief. "So it isn't the flu."

"No, but pneumonia is no trifling matter. Apparently he's had it for some time but neglected to get care." I recall the persistent cough that Georg had shrugged off in order to keep working. Ignoring their health is another way in which he and Papa are alike. "Anyway, they've pumped him full of medicine and he should be discharged to his rooms later today."

We round the corner, skirting the edge of the market, where chickens and cabbage and fabric and tools are sold indiscriminately alongside one another from wooden, tarp-covered stalls or cloths spread on the ground. The smell of fish, still alive in murky tubs of water, hangs heavy in the air. Krysia lowers her voice to a whisper. "I spoke with Ignatz after the reception last night," she says, and I understand then her reason for coming here in person rather than ringing. "I thought perhaps I could reason with him, but I was wrong. He's quite dangerous. He came from the Pale, saw his own brother murdered by the czar's army." He had lost a brother like Georg, but he had responded with anger and bile. "He has a criminal past, has done things that I'd rather not know about. In another time, he would be just a common thug. But in this world…" I nod. Paris right now is a free-for-all, the old rules broken. Power and opportunity are there for those who dare take it.

"Perhaps I should just refuse. After all, Papa has been given an ambassadorial title for purposes of the conference. With his diplomatic immunity, surely he would be sheltered from any scandal."

She shakes her head. "I grew up as a diplomat's child, remember? Immunity is easily dispensed with for political purposes. If your father was found to have leaked information, he could be arrested, or simply declared persona non grata and ordered to leave the country." I nod. Even if he weren't formally prosecuted, the scandal and having to face Uncle Walter in failure would be more than Papa could bear. "Ignatz isn't going to let you off until he gets what he wants."

"But I haven't seen any documents," I say evasively. "Georg only has me work on translations, documents given to him by the English or the French. They're nothing like the information on German weapons that Ignatz wanted. Perhaps Georg doesn't even know anything."

"He's a senior military officer and a member of the delegation," she replies impatiently. "Of course he knows something. And now…"

"He's sick."

She swats at a gnat, then exhales, exasperated. "So much the better. He'll be resting, disoriented."

"I'm not going to take advantage of his condition." There is a line I won't cross, even when threatened.

"Why are you protecting him? Is it because you have feelings for him?"

"No, of course not. I'm engaged," I add, pulling Stefan's ring from my pocket and holding it up like some sort of amulet to ward off danger. "But Georg trusts me."

"So does your father," she adds pointedly.

My stomach tightens. How had I gotten into such a mess? But Krysia is right. My loyalties must lie with Papa.

"You asked for my help and I've done what I can. You need to look out for yourself now." She kisses me on the cheek. "I have to go. Come see me when you are in the city."

"Wait…" She turns back expectantly. I search for the words to form a question, and seek extra guidance from her. But I must figure out the rest on my own. "Thank you."

"Not at all. I wish I could have been more help. Take care of yourself. Get some rest. And here…." She reaches in her bag and pulls out a small sachet. "You might give these to Georg in some tea or broth." She knows, even before I've admitted it to myself, that I will be going to him.

"What is it?"

"Just herbs, rose hips and such. They are most restorative." She presses the sachet into my hands and, before I can thank her again, turns and walks down the street.

I return to our apartment where the tea I'd made earlier still sits on the table. I pick up the semi-warm cup, thinking back to my walk in the garden with Georg the previous evening. There had never been a moment like that with me and Stefan. It is hardly a fair comparison, since we knew each other our entire lives before we were together.

But even if we had been strangers and met under similar circumstances, it would feel nothing like this. Stefan. Sometimes it is as if he is already gone. But he is out there, wounded yet alive. And I am, or am supposed to be, his.

Papa emerges from his room, dressed for the conference session in the city. "I'm afraid there's a meeting tonight, so I won't be back to dine with you. Would you care to come into the city today? You could shop with Celia."

"I'll just stay here, if you don't mind. I'm quite tired after last night's dinner."

His eyebrows lift. Then he shrugs. "It's your choice. I just thought, now that your work with Georg is on hiatus, you might be bored."

I set the teacup down. "Krysia told me that he's to be released from the hospital today."

"He's sick, darling. He won't be able to work. And surely you aren't thinking about going over there…."

"It's pneumonia, Papa," I answer quickly. "Not contagious at all."

"You can't be certain." But then, seeing my stubborn expression he knows so well, he shrugs. "My car is waiting. Don't stay too long at the hotel."

"I won't," I promise.

"Be careful—and give him my best."

When the door has closed behind him, I race to the window, craning my neck to look down the street at the hotel. It could be hours before Georg returns. I straighten the apartment, then sit down to read by the window. But I glance up to check the street so often I cannot keep my place. Finally, I give up and pace the apartment restlessly.

It is late afternoon when I finally glimpse a flash of white, the top of an ambulance as it lumbers down the cobblestone street below. I leap to my feet in time to see the back doors of the ambulance opening in front of the hotel. My heart twists as Georg is carried motionless on a stretcher through the front gate. When the ambulance has disappeared again, I go to the washroom to freshen. Then, unable to wait any longer, I make my way down to the street. The guard at the front of the hotel, accustomed to my late-day arrival, nods as I pass.

I knock on the door to Georg's apartment and a moment later it swings open, revealing an attractive dark-haired girl wearing a white apron and cap. *"Oui?"*

"Oh." I falter. It had not occurred to me that anyone would be here. It makes sense—Georg is helpless and needs care. Still, I cannot help resent the familiar way the nurse moves around his room, the ease with which she adjusts his pillow.

From the hulking mass of blankets atop the bed, there comes a violent cough. "Georg?" As I move toward him, my jealousy is replaced with concern. He lies motionless with eyes closed, his skin damp and gray. Was he really well enough to be discharged?

His eyes flutter open and as they focus on me, he smiles faintly. "Margot…" He struggles to sit up.

I press my hand on his shoulder. "Rest, and don't try to move."

He nods slightly in acquiescence, then closes his eyes once more. There is a dark stubble about his cheeks which gives him an unkempt look. Trying not to stare at the top of his chest, the few dark hairs revealed by the open collar of his dressing gown, I avert my gaze. The apartment is tidy, but there are smells of antiseptic and iodine I do not recognize.

He opens his eyes again. "Hello," he says, as though he had forgotten I was there. His faint smile lifts my heart. "Now if you will help me get out of this silly bed, we can get back to work."

"Work? You can't possibly work in your condition."

Frustration crosses his face as he processes for the first time the delay that his incapacitation will cause. "How could I have allowed this to happen?"

"You're human. Humans get ill."

He shakes his head stubbornly. "Not me. Not now."

I take his hand, rubbing it like a child's to soothe him. "Shh. Getting upset will only make things worse."

The nurse appears again and sets down a tray of broth and toast on the nightstand by the bed. "*Merci,* Mildred. That will be all," George says.

"But…" She looks confused at being dismissed. "There's a tonic if he starts feeling poorly. I'll check on him again in the morning.

"The delegation insisted upon hiring her," he explains when she has gone. He coughs again, the spasms indicating that he is the furthest thing from better.

"Drink," I order, holding the cup and supporting his head. His hair where it meets his neck is short, like the fuzz of a baby chick I once held.

"It's awful," he says when he has recovered, frowning so hard I wonder if he is in pain. "You seeing me like this."

"Not at all." But his expression remains displeased. Does he mind that I have come? "I was so worried…" His eyes widen, as if unused to having anyone care about him. "Do you want me to go?"

"No," he replies firmly, almost before I have finished asking. "But if you could help me…" I lean forward in anticipation of his request, another pillow or perhaps some medicine. "Can you bring me my binder from the desk?"

"You aren't nearly well enough to work," I insist again.

"But there's no time." He tries to sit up.

I press him back against the pillow firmly, the skin of his bare chest warm under my hand. "If you get up too soon and relapse, we'll never finish."

"But—"

"I can keep working for you," I interrupt. He relaxes, seemingly mollified. I walk to the anteroom and retrieve the binder he'd indicated and carry it back. "Now I will keep translating as long as you rest. Understood?"

He smiles weakly and closes his eyes once more. "Yes, *fraulein*."

I shift in the hardwood chair, balancing the binder on my lap. Working like this is awkward, but I can watch him from here in case he needs anything. A fan hums low in the corner, sending the curtains dancing a gentle waltz. I glance up. Georg's head is tilted back and he is snoring lightly, eyes dancing beneath their lids. What does he dream about? His features are so familiar to me now, the way Stefan's should have been, if only I could remember them clearly. His face is relaxed, as vulnerable and innocent as a boy's. My heart twists. Here I am, caring for Georg as I should have been

Stefan. But this does not feel suffocating—I belong here and this is where I want to be.

An hour passes. I set down the translation. Georg is awake now and watching me. "How are you?"

"A bit better now, I think."

"Do you want to try some of the broth?" He nods. I move the tray close and start to spoon it for him.

"I can manage." I sit back, watching as he eats with a shaky hand.

He eats in silence, his eyes focused over my shoulder. I follow his gaze to a picture of a group of men on the deck of an enormous ship. "Are you thinking of the sea?"

"The men. They called me a hero after Jutland," he said. "But I just did what was expected of me, and we—most of us, anyway—made it through. Later I was summoned from the ship to the delegation. The sailors—they think I abandoned them." He sets the spoon down as a pained look crosses his face.

"Shh," I soothe.

He continues, as if he has not heard me. "I'm so broken, Margot. And if I can make this work…" His eyes are desperate, wild. He clings to his work for the conference like a raft. "When I'm with you, it all seems possible somehow." My stomach flips. "The day I stepped off that bus and saw you standing by the roadside, I felt as if I had somehow known you my whole life." Can he possibly be saying such things? I search his face but his eyes are glazed, lost in some sort of delirium.

I reach forward and press my hand to his forehead. It is alarmingly hot, his fever climbing as night approaches. Perhaps it was a mistake to let the nurse leave. I walk to the sink and find the tonic she'd indicated. "Swallow," I order, holding a spoonful of the thick brown syrup to his lips.

He obeys, grimacing. "Talk to me…." He pants, eyes closed, too sick now to care whether I continue working or not. "I should like to have a dog again," he remarks sleepily, jumping topics without reason. "A terrier, most likely."

"Yes," I say, a mother giving permission for such a pet. He reaches for my hand and I let him take it. This will mean nothing, I tell myself. But there is an intensity to his touch and longing rises in me before I can help it.

"The other day, when I told you there had never been a woman…that wasn't entirely true." I hold my breath. "There was someone once. At port in Genoa, I met a young woman." I close my eyes, desperately curious and at the same time wishing he would not continue. "We walked the city and she showed me a great many sites before bidding me bon voyage. She took me as just another sailor, though I could have liked her quite a bit." The book that is Georg opens and words spill forth, forming a picture that I can now see more completely.

"You remind me of her." I stiffen. I do not want to be a substitute for someone else. "She was just an image, there for a few hours. But I've gotten to know you so much more. The way you flare your nostrils when angry." I cringe at this less-than-flattering description. "How your eyes seem to change colors with your temper, like two mood stones…" These last words slur as he starts to drift off. Conflicting emotions rise up in me—jealousy over this woman that once held his heart and relief that he has cared, is capable of it.

He does not speak further. I pick up the binder once more, but I am unable to concentrate. Georg is sleeping deeply now, a snore like a low growl each time he inhales, a whistle more teakettle than train with every release. My thoughts turn to Ignatz and the need to find something to pacify him. But the kind of information Ignatz seeks, if Georg possesses it at all, would not be found in the documents that Georg has me translate. I look toward the study, Krysia's suggestion to search while he is asleep echoing in my mind. If I am going to do this it has to be now. I will check, just once, in order to satisfy Ignatz that there is nothing here. I open the door to the sitting room, then turn back, my guilt rising at the sight of Georg sleeping peacefully. I do not want to betray his trust, but I have to protect Papa.

Trying to step normally but keep my footsteps quiet, I walk through the doorway. On the far side of the sitting room, there is a stack of documents he keeps separate from the other papers, the ones he asks me to translate. I pick up the pile and riffle through, scanning the documents, which are in German. There are cables here about shipbuilding operations, a new line of cargo freighters. I relax slightly. So this is why he has not asked me to translate these materials—they pertain not at all to the conference, but rather to his family's shipping business.

I turn to the next page and stop, my hand suspended midair. It contains technical engineering plans and though the terminology is foreign to me, it is clearly a plan to fit the cargo ships with guns. A shiver runs through me. Was all Georg's talk of peace a lie, intended for my benefit? I continue paging through, then stop at a map. Cities to the east are marked: Archangel, Murmansk, Brest. Though I do not understand the notations, I know this is what Ignatz wanted.

I remove the document from the stack, my hand trembling slightly. I'd done it. In the other room Georg snores, none the wiser. I am flooded with remorse. Georg is so earnest and he has brought me into his trust. I've betrayed him.

Georg cries out then in his sleep, a whimper that breaks open to a scream. I fold the paper hurriedly and tuck it in my dress. With any luck I can show it to Ignatz and return it before Georg notices that it is missing.

Back in the bedroom, Georg is agitated in his sleep. He is on the ship, reliving a battle as his body convulses from side to side—most likely the one that had taken his brother. Sitting on the edge of the bed, I throw my arms around him. His gown is soaked through with sweat, skin hot through the material. "I'm here and it's okay." He wraps himself around me, holding me tightly as though I might slip away.

A minute later, his grip relaxes and he begins to breathe evenly once more. I look at the clock on the nightstand. It is nearly eleven, and Papa might be back from his dinner, if he did not go to Celia's. He will wonder where I've gone, but I cannot leave Georg and there's no way to send word. I lean back wearily beside him on the wide bed.

I awaken sometime later. Where am I? Georg's rooms, I remember, inhaling the familiar spearmint smell of his aftershave. I had not planned to fall asleep. The room clicks into focus as my eyes adjust to the darkness. I sit up quickly.

He shifts beside me, opens his eyes. "Margot." He smiles, his face as relaxed and happy as I have ever seen. "You are here. I thought it was a dream." He blinks. "Were you here all night?"

"Yes." I study his face. Does he recall the things he said? But his expression is impassive, the awkwardness that would have been present if he remembered his declaration of feelings nowhere to be found.

Then his face clouds. "How improper of me. I never should have…"

"It's fine. I came to you. It was my choice. I wanted to be here."

Then a pained look crosses his face as his head begins to throb, bringing the memories of the previous evening into focus. "I'm so sorry. You should not have had to see me in such a state. You should go."

He does not want me here. Stung by his curtness, I stand and start for the door. "Margot, wait." He grabs my hand to stop me. I am instantly warm. What is it about this man that provokes such a reaction in me? It was never this way with Stefan, no matter how much I liked him.

Then he drops my hand just as quickly. "It's just that when I sleep…" He turns away, embarrassed.

"I have nightmares, too," I say, wanting to ease his embarrassment. "Not about anything as serious as yours, of course."

"What do you dream about?" Before he finished the

question, I realize my mistake: I cannot tell him about the fiancé and the inevitable marriage that haunts my sleep.

"I dream that I am trapped," I say carefully, somewhere short of a lie. I hold my breath hoping that he will not press me to elaborate. "How are you feeling?" I ask, changing the subject.

"Much better."

I touch his now-cool forehead. "The nurse said she would check back on you this morning."

"You should go home and rest."

Or at least wash. My hair is pressed flat to my head from sleep and I have a stale taste in my mouth.

"If I may trouble you for one thing before you go, I should like to shave." I notice then the thick stubble that covers his cheeks. He is not used to being so unkempt.

"Certainly." I fetch a bowl of warm water and his shaving kit from the basin. When I return to Georg's beside, he has unbuttoned the collar of his nightshirt further, revealing a wide swath of skin. Warmth rises in me. He drapes his neck in a towel and dampens his face. But as he reaches for the razor, his weakened hand trembles. "Let me." I work the cream into a lather as I have seen Papa do, then bring my hands to his cheeks. His skin is unexpectedly soft beneath my fingertips. I run the razor upward against his jawline, struggling to keep my hand still, not meeting his eyes.

"Much better," he says when I have rinsed the lather. He pats his face dry with the towel I hand him. "Thank you."

"Not at all." I still cannot look at him.

"Margot, I am so grateful for your friendship." I step back, caught off guard by the word. "I'm sorry, was that too forward of me? We've known each other for such a short time."

"Not at all." To the contrary, his description sounded cold and formal, something well short of how I feel. He does not consider me more. Of course not. Whatever was I expecting?

"I don't think of it as you working for me, you see. I regard us as peers, colleagues, but the way we speak of so many things makes it something more than that...." He fumbles with these last words, then clears his throat. "Now, if you'll bring me my papers."

"You're still too sick. That was our arrangement, remember? I shall keep working as long as you rest."

"Yes, but now you are going."

He has a point. I need to return to the apartment to freshen and make sure Papa is not worried. "I hate being idle like this," he presses. "There isn't any time to waste. Every day that passes decreases the chance of getting the report to the commission and making a real difference."

"I can keep working," I offer quickly. Then I stop. "I mean, not here, of course, but if I take the papers with me."

I watch as he considers the idea. The delegation is worried about material slipping out, concerns about espionage growing by the day, though whether legitimate or just paranoia it is impossible to say. Papa has told me before that they even play the gramophone as they work, symphonies and operas at a decibel that makes it hard to think, to prevent anyone from listening. "I'll take them from here to our rooms and nowhere else," I promise. "I'll bring them back tonight."

"I suppose your suite really is just an extension of the delegation space here," Georg concedes. I wait for him to admonish me to be careful. But he doesn't. He trusts me, something which I suspect does not come easily to him. Something I do not deserve.

"I will check on you later. Stay in bed and rest. I can show myself out." I slip from the apartment before he has the chance to argue, taking the binder with me.

A few minutes later, I unlock the door to our apartment. The sitting room is still, I note with relief, untouched since the previous day. It is the first time I have ever been glad that Papa had spent the night with Celia. I set the binder on the desk then pull out the map I'd taken from Georg's rooms out of my dress. Will it be enough to satisfy Ignatz?

I place the document in the middle of the stack of papers in the binder, then walk to the toilet to wash. As I dress twenty minutes later, I glance over at my bed, the rose duvet bathed in sunlight. I am tired from my night of caring for Georg and the pillow beckons invitingly. But I promised Georg I would keep working.

I put on the kettle in the small kitchenette and a moment later return to the parlor with a cup of tea, which I set down on the low table by the divan before sitting. I pull out the sachet of herbs Krysia gave me the previous day for energy. I'd forgotten to put them in Georg's broth, but perhaps they will give me a bit of energy, as well. I tap a bit into the teacup, savoring the floral smell that wafts upward. I take a sip, then turn to the binder and remove the documents. But as I start on one of the memos, the words blur, making it difficult to read. I blink several times and take another sip of tea. I rub at my dry eyes, then set the papers down. Perhaps just a quick rest. I tilt my head back.

I sit up with a start, disoriented by flashes of dreams, dark scenes of the ocean, reaching for Georg's hand before sinking below the rough surf. How much time has passed? I struggle to adjust my eyes to the dim room. Though I had meant to rest only a few minutes, I can tell by the heaviness of my limbs and the way the scant late-afternoon light filters through the curtains that it has been hours.

The binder has fallen from my lap to the floor, documents scattering everywhere. How careless of me. I take the papers and fold them neatly back in the stack. I'd meant to go find Ignatz this afternoon and show him the report so that I could return it to Georg's study this evening, but it is too late now. I reach into the middle of the binder for the loose document I'd hidden there. As my hand closes around emptiness, my stomach tightens. Hurriedly, I page to the middle of the binder.

The report I'd stolen from Georg is gone.

9

I stare down at the binder in disbelief, paging through the documents a second, then a third time. The map had been there, I am sure of it. I retrace my route from when I entered the apartment, looking under the divan and table. But it is gone. I race to the window. Could it possibly have fallen in the street? I thought I had been so careful.

I put on my shoes and start for the door. But before I can turn the knob, it opens from the other side and standing there, glowering, is Papa. "There you are!" he exclaims, nostrils flaring as he enters the apartment. I have never seen him so angry. "I tried to ring you last night and then again early this morning and finally was so worried that I came to check as soon as I was able. You were at the hotel, weren't you?"

"Papa, I…" I search for another explanation that would explain my absence at such hours and find none.

"I knew it! You said you were just checking on Captain Richwalder briefly."

"I hadn't planned to stay. But he was so sick, and there was no one else to help."

"And then walking out of the hotel the next morning, like some…I cannot even say. It isn't proper."

"Is that what matters now? It was a very urgent circumstance."

But he is too far gone to back down. "What will the other members of the delegation think?" His voice raises and a vein stands out on the left side of his head.

I should hope that the other delegates have more important things to worry about than my comings and goings, I want to say. Papa has never been one to trouble about appearances, but his tenuous position here at the conference has made him subject to scrutiny. "Papa, your pressure," I remind him instead, alarmed that the fight will be too much strain on his health. "I'm sorry I worried you," I add, trying to calm him.

"Working for Captain Richwalder on some translations is one thing." His tone softens slightly. "But staying out all night and playing nursemaid…"

"Papa, I'm not a child."

"Exactly. And I expect you to make adult decisions." Or if not, decisions will be made for me, is the silent, unfinished implication. For years, Papa has encouraged me to think on my own, but now I see that is intended to go only so far, like an animal perceiving it has free rein because it has not comprehended the contours of its cage. "Spending time with Georg when you are an engaged woman. It isn't proper," he repeats.

"And you and Tante Celia," I spit, unable to hold back. "Is that proper?" He blinks and his cheeks flush as though I have slapped him.

"I'm not…" He stops short, unable to finish the denial. "That's entirely different." But my recriminations hang in the air between us. In all of the years the affair has gone on, it is the first time either of us has spoken of it.

A moment later, he clears his throat. "I have to return to Paris for dinner now that I know you are all right. You are to stay here."

"I'll not be a prisoner."

"That's rather dramatic. You can leave the apartment. But you aren't to go to Captain Richwalder."

I start to protest. "Papa..." He goes to his room and closes the door hard. I stare after him, defeated. How can he possibly tell me I cannot continue to work with Georg, or to see him when he is ill? And then to assume how I feel.... Papa has always tried to guide with a gentle touch. But this seems to be the one exception.

I walk from the apartment, then hesitate. For a minute I consider defying Papa's order and going back to Georg. Suddenly this has become a power struggle. What will happen if I refuse to listen? I am an adult, after all, and a person of my own accord. Papa could turn me out like Krysia's parents initially did when she became pregnant. For all of the conflict, though, he has no wish to alienate me. He could make trouble for Georg with the delegation. But Papa isn't the type to make waves. No, there is not likely to be any tangible repercussions from my going against his will. Still, fighting with him even for a few minutes makes me ill.

Remembering the lost document, I hurry down the street, check the gutters and the scraps of newspaper that blow along the roadside. It is nowhere to be found. What now?

Krysia. She will know what to do. I start in the direction

of the train station. It is nearly dark outside now, the shops closing. At the end of the street, I gaze back longingly at the hotel. Georg will be waiting for me, wonder why I have not come. I walk to the guard at the front of the hotel and scribble a note for Georg, making my excuses.

An hour later, I ring the bell at the entrance to Krysia's apartment building. When I reach the top of the stairs, the door opens and Krysia appears in a long flowing robe.

"I'm so sorry. I should have called," I add, repeating our now-familiar refrain without humor.

"I think we're long past that," she replies wryly. Then, noticing my distress, her face grows serious. "What is it?" I twist my hands reflexively around my purse, embarrassed to be running to Krysia with my problems yet again. "Come in."

Inside, I scan the apartment warily, relieved to see that Marcin is not there. Krysia does not prepare coffee as she usually does but instead, sensing the need for something stronger, pulls a bottle of brandy and pours small amounts into two glasses. "Drink," she orders when I look at her hesitantly. I obey, the strong liquor burning my nose and throat. "Now," she says, "what's wrong?"

Hurriedly, I tell her about taking the document. "I tried to do what Ignatz wanted. Only now it's missing."

"You searched your apartment?"

"I looked everywhere."

"It will turn up. These things do." She seems strangely untroubled.

"Perhaps I should tell Georg…."

"No," she replies quickly. "Do you really think he would

understand?" She's right, of course. Telling him would mean revealing my deception and he would never forgive me. "There's still time for you to try again and get something else."

"Again?" I explode. I cannot help it. Taking from Georg once was bad enough. But the thought of doing it a second time... "I can't."

"We've been through this before. There's no other way."

"But betraying him like this when he trusts me...I feel horrid."

She raises an eyebrow. "You care for him."

"Hardly." My voice raises a note too high in protest. "We disagree about everything." I search my memory to find an example. "Like the other day we fought about Palestine."

"He didn't see the need for a Jewish state?"

"No, quite the opposite actually. He thought it would be good for the Jews to have a place. But I am a German and I didn't see the necessity." It sounds so trivial now. What is it about Georg that brings out such a strong reaction in me? "What do you think?"

"About Palestine? I believe that Jews enjoy relative calm and stability in Europe right now. Especially in places like Germany." I nod in agreement. Back home we are integrated into almost every part of society, academics like Papa, businessmen like Uncle Walter. "But in the East, where I come from, it wasn't always that way. There were these terrible pogroms where the Jews were forced from villages at best or even beaten or killed, their homes burned, often with no notice at all. In recent years there have been sudden outbursts of violence, even where the Jews had lived peacefully among their neighbors for centuries. I think that's why so many of them don't mind the communists—it has to be better than what they suffered under the czars."

I try to imagine the violence of the world Krysia described. Poland is Germany's eastern neighbor again, or will be now that it has been re-created at the conference. The places where this happened are just hundreds of miles from Berlin, but the barbarity is so foreign it might have taken place centuries ago.

"I suppose it really doesn't matter what we quarreled about," I say, returning to the subject of Georg in spite of myself. "We just don't see eye to eye on anything."

"Why should you? You've got nothing in common."

Is that true? Our backgrounds are quite dissimilar. Yet there is a connection between Georg and me when we speak that makes all of the differences disappear. "I don't know about that, exactly," I say slowly. "He's just so stubborn."

She let out a chuckle, uncharacteristically abrupt, almost a snort. "You're rather headstrong yourself, my dear. And that's a good thing. Headstrong holds its own in a head-wind, my grandmother used to say."

"Maybe that's why we argue so much."

"Maybe. Or maybe it's because you like him," she says again.

I stop drinking midmouthful, heedless of the brandy that lingers on my tongue, burning. "Like him?" I repeat the words, buying time in which to formulate a real response.

"Or is this just about rebellion? Because there are easier ways…"

I consider the question. I can see how it might seem that

way—a girl from a well-to-do family, rearing back against expectations. Indeed, when Papa and I quarreled my first instinct was to run to Georg. But my feelings for Georg aren't about that—they are real and I would care as much if Papa approved and he fit neatly into my world.

"It isn't that. But how can I possibly have feelings for a man I've known less than a week?"

She shrugs. "Sometimes you just know," and her tone suggests the observation is personal. But is she talking about Marcin or the man who came before and gave her Emilie?

"Even if I did, it's a moot point. He thinks of me as a silly child."

She dipped her head. "One could get in much trouble for looking at a child like that."

"What do you mean?"

"You can see a great deal from the piano bench. Georg watches you with real feeling—and an intensity I've seldom seen."

"It doesn't matter," I insist. "There's no future in it."

"Because of your fiancé? Engagements can be broken. It isn't that hard."

"No, you don't understand. It's so much worse." I pause, and take a deep breath. "Krysia, I'm married!" I bring my hand to my mouth. It is the first time I've confessed this to anyone, the secret I've pushed so far from my mind these recent months. But spoken aloud now, the words are now real, impossible to deny.

The evening before Stefan was to report for duty we'd gone down to the Unter den Linden. It was a humid August evening and a fine coat of perspiration covered everything.

The street was closely packed with revelers, celebrating Germany's certain quick victory, men and women such as ourselves enjoying a last night together in the cafés and dance halls before the men left for war. Outside the Rathaus, a line had formed. A few of the women clutched makeshift bouquets of flowers or Bibles.

"They're waiting to get married," Stefan observed, a note of prompting to his voice. I did not respond. The couples were mostly working class, with their simple dresses and worn coats. Those women sorely needed the benefits that came with being a soldier's wife—or a soldier's widow if things went wrong. I was lucky enough to have not just Papa, but the security of Uncle Walter and the family estate to fall back on. I would be sad, but not destitute, if Stefan should fall.

But as Stefan watched the queue inch toward the town hall, there was a light in his eyes like none I had seen before. "Should we…?" He could not bring himself to finish the question and behind the hope, the fear of rejection flickered.

I hesitated. There were a dozen reasons to decline: I wanted a real wedding (the furthest thing from the truth), I could not get married without Papa being there. Seeing Stefan's face, though, I knew that he needed this if he was to make it through whatever lay ahead. "Let's." Hand in hand we walked toward the courthouse to be married.

The line progressed up the steps of the town hall, couples pressed close behind us. In front of us a woman leaned in and rested her head contentedly on her fiancé's shoulder. Something prickled at me. It was not right. It was all happening too fast. I wanted to tell Stefan that we should wait and do this another time with our families, but he stared straight ahead, shoulders squared, chin lifted with confidence. My palms began to sweat and I wondered if he would notice and ask me what was wrong. He squeezed my hand, oblivious.

Minutes passed, seeming like hours. As we neared the front of the room, a tight grip closed around my chest until I could not breathe. I turned, pulling my hand from Stefan's and searching for the exit. But it was too late—the registrant was taking down our names on a piece of paper and completing the certificate. I could scarcely hear the question she asked over the buzzing in my ears. *"Ja,"* I croaked. Then it was over and we were shuffled to the side to make way for the next couple.

"That's it?" I asked. I had not been a woman who had dreamed of a wedding ceremony, but it was hard to believe that a few words and signatures were the difference between freedom and forever.

"Yes?" His smile dampened. "You don't mind, do you? We'll do the rest after." Armed with our marriage, he could go off to war believing in *after.* "Unless you want to tell our families?"

"No." The word came out more firmly than I'd intended. "Papa would be upset not to be here."

"This should have been so much more," Stefan lamented as we walked down the steps of the Rathaus. "I'm happy we did it, of course. But you deserve a proper wedding, with a reception after."

I shook my head. "Nonsense. You know I've never cared about that. The marriage is what's important, being yours."

But a lump grew in my throat as I clutched tighter the piece of paper that bound me to him. Something did not feel right, like a rock caught in one's shoe, pressing down painfully step after step. It was not the lack of a wedding I minded. Rather, the permanency of what we had just done crashed onto me.

After dinner we returned to our house to find a surprise party, a gathering of family and close friends. "A small celebration," Papa said.

He knows! I thought with alarm, wondering if he and Stefan discussed a quick wedding, as well as our engagement. "Since there is no time for an engagement party," he added.

My shoulders slumped with relief. *Oh, Papa*, I thought as he raised a glass and said a few quiet words about me and Stefan, love and hope. *If only you knew.* My heart ached to tell him. We never had secrets when I was a child. "You didn't have to do this," I said instead. "It is really too kind."

"These happy moments are rare, and to be rarer still in the months to come," he replied. There was a darkness behind his eyes that hinted at his true suspicions about the war, that nothing would be as sure and quick as the politicians and journalists were making out. Papa studied war for a living, centuries and centuries of fighting since the Mongols and the Tartars. He knew that if it were really so easy, the war would not have been fought at all but resolved another way.

"At least," Celia said coldly, "if something happens, you would have been engaged." She was not trying to be cruel, just practical. To her, having had someone who really wanted you, enough to make it official, meant everything.

What would she have said if she knew the truth about our already-marriage? She surely would have been embarrassed by the crude nature of our courthouse wedding.

"If only we hadn't gone to the courthouse that day," I say, as I finish telling Krysia. "This would have all been so much easier to untangle without the lies. And I'm sorry I didn't tell you earlier. But you see now why Georg and I can never be together."

"Marriage isn't a death sentence. People end marriages. Perhaps in this situation, where it isn't publicly known, it might be easier."

"Stefan would never agree. And even if he did, I couldn't do that to him now that he is hurt."

"Is lying to him any better?"

"It won't be a lie. Once I'm back in Berlin and we have the chance to get to know each other more intimately, I'm certain things will be different."

"You mean you and Stefan never consummated your marriage?"

I shake my head, feeling the blush creep up my neck. "There wasn't time."

Stefan had not come to me that night. I'd lain awake, wondering if he might slip up to my window and find a way for us to be together. We were, after all, married and this one chance to explore the things I'd only read about secretly was perhaps the brightest spot in all of this. "I've got to report at five tomorrow," he'd murmured as he left. "And we should wait until we're properly married by a rabbi, anyway, rather than sneaking around."

Krysia gives a soft laugh. "What?" I demand angrily.

"I'm sorry, my dear. I'm not making light of your situation, not in the slightest. But you aren't married, not in the biblical sense. Even the church might annul a marriage under such circumstances."

"To Stefan we are." And I've never heard of an annulment in Judaism, I lament silently.

"Do you really believe you can just go back to the old life and fit in so easily as though none of this ever happened?" She has a point. I'm not the same girl I was four years ago. "Life has a way of reshaping us." I'm unsure if she is talking about herself or me.

"Anyway, I'm sure you're wrong." I wave away the bottle of brandy she's picked up again, but she ignores me and pours. "Georg isn't interested in me. I'm a diversion, that's all."

"You're attractive and intelligent and articulate. Why do you discount yourself? It's a defense mechanism, I think, to protect yourself from rejection," she says, answering her own question. "Don't let anyone get close and they won't leave or be able to hurt you again. Maybe it's because of your mother." She is not being unkind, just speaking bluntly. "Death is a kind of abandonment," she adds.

"Anyway, Georg and Stefan are two separate issues," she continues, raising her hands in opposite directions. "Your feelings for Stefan changed long before Georg came along." But even if I had truly been in love with Stefan, I would have noticed Georg—no matter what. Georg did not cause me to stop loving Stefan. But he highlighted the difference between everything and emptiness and made it impossible for me to go back to a place where the latter was enough.

"Did you love Stefan? Ever, I mean?"

I consider the question. "I think so. I mean, I was so lonely and well, being with Stefan was company."

"There are worse things than being alone."

"I don't like Georg," I protest again. "He's all wrong for me."

"Yet you haven't told him about Stefan?"

I shake my head. "Not exactly." Why hadn't I told Georg the truth about Stefan? Now, of course, it would be awkward, a secret kept too long. But back at the very beginning when we were discussing our childhoods and families and lives back home as the newest of acquaintances might, it would have been the most natural thing in the world to mention. It was more than just my guilt over the fact that I am here in Paris while Stefan convalesces in a veteran's hospital. No, there was something about Georg right from the start that made me want to keep that part of myself hidden.

"Georg isn't the man for me," I repeat stubbornly.

"Nor is Stefan," she adds with a certainty that makes me wonder if she has met him. I look at her, puzzled. "You have no warmth when you speak about him."

"No," I admit, unable to lie to her. "It's not because he's injured. It's as though the light has gone out in the furnace inside me with respect to Stefan, and much as I try to blow on it, I can't make the embers burn. Perhaps it's because I haven't seen him in four years." My eyes begin to water. "I can barely picture his face."

"Or because you were sixteen when you became engaged, scarcely more than a child." She's right. The girl I was before the war was someone I barely remember. "We commit our lives to others when we are still unformed ourselves. I'm glad I met Marcin later—it would not have been the same when we were young. We had to make our mistakes."

But neither Krysia's explanation of age nor mine of the passage of time adequately explains my lack of warmth for Stefan. He is wrong for me. The way I feel when I am with Georg has changed my notion of love and made it impossible to go back to the bland feelings I once had for Stefan.

"What am I going to do?" Tears fill my eyes. Krysia reaches out and pulls me close, her arms warmer than I could have imagined, like the mother's touch I have lacked for so long. I put my head in her lap and weep like a child.

"There, there." Krysia's voice is a warm blanket, her advice wise—like a big sister I never had, or the mother I scarcely knew.

A few minutes later, I sit up and wipe my eyes. "I'm so sorry."

"Don't be. Emotion is human—and good for us. It shows that we care. It is getting late, though," Krysia remarks.

I glance at the clock on the mantel. It is almost eleven. "I'm so sorry," I repeat, standing to leave. I have overstayed my welcome. "I should go."

But she shakes her head, pulls me gently back to the settee. "Not at all. You won't get a taxi this time of night and the trains will have stopped running. Why don't you just stay here? It's nothing posh, but you're most welcome. Marcin is playing an engagement out of the city."

My shoulders sag with exhaustion. Suddenly staying in

Krysia's warm apartment seems the most inviting thing in the world. "Thank you."

"Your father won't be worried? There's a telephone booth at the corner."

"Oh." I would rather not speak with Papa after our quarrel, but I don't dare to go missing a second night.

"Why don't I run down and ring him while you freshen up?" she offers, sensing my unease. Gratefully, I scribble down the number on the back of the matchbook she hands me. "The toilet is just down the hall if you need it."

When I return to the apartment a few minutes later, Krysia has fixed up some blankets and a pillow on the divan. "There." I burrow under, inhaling the scent of her perfume and looking around the room in the darkness.

"You don't have a piano to play here," I say, noticing for the first time, as my eyes grow heavy. Of course not. There would have been no way to get it to the garret and no room for it, anyway. No phonograph or radio, either. It seems the oddest thing for a musician to have no music.

"No. There's a music store around the corner that lets me play theirs in exchange for giving the occasional lesson."

"I like quiet," she says, reading my thoughts. "You shouldn't be afraid to be alone with your own thoughts." She dims the lamp, then retreats to the loft bed in the corner of the flat without speaking further, as if to prove a point.

Surrounded by the soft downy bedding and Krysia's lilac scent, I drift quickly to sleep. I dream that I am running down the street from our apartment to the hotel in Versailles, searching for something, perhaps the missing document. No, not something, I realize as I reach the hotel.

Someone. I am late for work and I go into Georg's hotel room but the bed is made, all of his personal effects gone, and it is as if he was never here at all. I turn and suddenly it is not his hotel room at all but our house back in Berlin and I reach for the doorknob but it will not open. I am trapped.

My eyes fly open. I blink in the darkness, confused. Krysia's apartment, I remember, hearing her faint snore. I lay awake, shaken and trying to collect fragments of the dream as they scatter.

My thoughts turn to our earlier conversation, my revelation to Krysia that Stefan and I are already wed. What is marriage, anyway? It has been over four years since Stefan and I went to the Rathaus and came out with that piece of paper callings us man and wife, and yet I feel no closer to him than the stranger I pass on the street. Was it supposed to confer some new feeling, or simply recognize what is already there? But if it is no more than acknowledgment of the status quo, then why do we need it at all?

Sometimes it is as if I have two people inside me—the one that knows what is right and the one that does not care and only knows want, desire. She is the one who would cast off these skirts and run wild through the forest, who would hop a freighter for China. My gaze travels to the window and the thin strip of night sky above the roofs of the buildings. I could just leave. I'd head west, I decide, over the rolling hills until I reach the sea and a ship to take me away from it all. How would I survive? I've never had a job, do not have any skills, but I could find work as a governess or tutor. Something tells me I can manage hard work, am perhaps even suited to it. And my needs are simple, a place to rest, a bit of food. But I could not leave Papa any more than I could forsake myself.

"There are some doors," Krysia told me once, "that are not meant to be opened." At the time she was referring to her own situation, my suggestion that she try to talk to Emilie. But remembering the day I met her, the words also ring true. What if I had stopped at the gate of the Jardin des Tuileries that December afternoon, heeded my inner warning and not gone through? I would not have gone to the café and spoken carelessly in front of her artist friends and I would not be embroiled in this whole mess with Ignatz. But then I also would not have known Krysia and she is so embedded in my world I can scarcely imagine it without her. No, it is impossible to take one piece of the puzzle away and try to envision the rest whole.

My eyelids grow heavy and I allow myself to be lulled to sleep once more by a gentle breeze through the open window and the sounds of the street below.

10

The next morning I awaken on the strange divan, still in my dress from the previous evening. My mouth is sour from the brandy. "Krysia?" The apartment is still, the sound of her snoring gone. On the table beside the couch sits a hastily scrawled note.

Had to run out on an errand. Meet me outside the station in Versailles today at noon.
—K

The note does not give the purpose of our meeting, nor does it contemplate the possibility of my being unavailable on such short notice.

Just before noon I stand at the entranceway to the Gare de Versailles-Chantiers, having returned home briefly to wash and change. The crowd at midday is a mix of locals making their way into the city. Suddenly I feel as if I am being watched. A chill creeps up my spine and I turn, scanning the travelers who move uneventfully from the ticket kiosk to the platform. It is paranoia, brought on by Ignatz and this spying business—the fear of getting caught, that he is somehow monitoring me all of the time.

In the distance, the cathedral clock begins to chime twelve. Perhaps Krysia isn't going to show. A moment later, I hear the sound of a car engine behind me. Krysia appears, not from the train platform as I thought she might, but through the stillness of the fog, resplendent and surreal, driving a motorcar, a long black Citroën, up the wide thoroughfare that runs perpendicular to the station. She wears a broad-brimmed hat, held by sashes tied under the chin that match perfectly the blue of her cape.

She pulls up to the curb but does not switch off the engine. "Come," she says, gesturing for me to get in the car.

"You can drive," I marvel.

She nods, concentrating as she pulls from the curb. "I can try."

"Where are we going?" She does not answer, but drives with both arms extended as though navigating a great ship as we follow the road that leads away from town. Soon the houses on the outskirts start to thin, giving way to the occasional farm. The fields, knee-high with too-dry crops and wildflowers, sway gently beneath the cloudless midday sky. "Beautiful," I remark. "So peaceful."

"So different now than during the war," Krysia agrees. "There were raids almost every night. Once Marcin and I were out walking and we had to hide in an arch at the Louvre." The war was so far away in London. It is hard to imagine being in the middle of it all.

We come to a roundabout and she follows it three-quarters of the way around, turning onto the spur that indicates towns to the northeast, the road toward Belgium. Great rolling fields of poppies flank either side of the road, an endless carpet of red.

An hour later, Krysia turns onto a smaller road, not much more than a country lane. Through the now-faded black paint that was used to cover the signs during the war, I can make out that we are headed in the direction of Reims. On a hill in the distance stand the remnants of the once-grand Reims cathedral. Though the tallest of its pillars still stands, the stained-glass windows are now jagged shards and its roof is peeled back like an open can.

Krysia slows as we approach the town center. In contrast to Paris or Versailles, Reims is a ghost town. Ours is the only motorcar on the narrow cobblestone street, which is deserted, save for a cart pulled by a sorry, malnourished mare. From the sidewalk, pedestrians eye us with interest. Here one can see the closeness of the war. Buildings the entire length of the street were destroyed by the bombs and only the front walls remain standing, gaping craters behind the facades, which seem ready to topple at any second. The smell of gunpowder hangs in the air as though the destruction took place hours, and not months or years, ago.

But there are small signs of life. At the end of the block, two low garage walls remain, standing opposite one another like bookends. A makeshift roof of canvas and oil paper has been erected between them, and a woman sells bread and fruit on the ground beneath. Krysia pulls the car to the curb and steps out to buy food from her. She hands the woman a fistful of bills, suggesting a desire to help rather than genuine hunger. A moment later, she returns with several fresh young peaches.

She hands me one, then starts the car again. I bite into the soft flesh, blotting at the juice that dribbles down my chin with a handkerchief. On the next block not even the fronts of the buildings remain, just low piles of rubble. *Abri—40 personnes* is painted on the foundation of one of the decimated buildings, indicating that shelter from bombs could safely be taken there, a promise broken.

The road leads us out of Reims and I breathe the air deeply, eager to clear the devastation from my lungs. The sky has begun to cloud over, dampness and fog chilling the air. We cross a low bridge, children wading in the stream beneath. Overhead, birds call to one another in seeming cadence with the car engine.

Krysia pulls to the side of the road and turns off the ignition. As I step from the car, moisture from the ankle-high grass seeps through my stockings and the heels of my boots sink deeper into the sodden earth with every step. A wind begins to blow, sweeping away the fog. We are standing in a rolling field that stretches to the horizon like a great wave before disappearing. It is a battlefield, or was. Now it is a graveyard. Small crosses, some painted white and others crudely handmade from sticks, spring up around our ankles like dandelions among the lush clover. A faint halo of mist lingers inches above the earth.

I stop midstep. I had avoided coming here, and might have demurred if Krysia had told me in advance where we were going. For even as I wanted to know everything, part of me had long suspected that I could not bear the truth. But I am here now and have no choice but to see.

We reach a row of trees that have been sheared at the

midpoint. Atop the amputated branches, new leaves have begun to sprout. Krysia unties her hat and removes it somberly. Her hair comes loose, billowing around her face as regal as a lion's mane.

I take a step forward. Krysia grabs my arm and pulls me back as I nearly step on something hard that juts from the earth. "Oh!" I gasp at the sight of naked bone.

She begins to walk up the hill. At the top of the ridge, the terrain that had appeared endless breaks suddenly. The trenches. The long tube of hollowed-out earth is much deeper and wider than I'd imagined, a kind of subterranean city where the men had lived and died, rats in a maze. The smell of peat and earth and human waste wafts upward. About fifty meters to our right, the trench is bisected abruptly by a great crater, maybe ninety feet in diameter. Like the spot where Stefan had nearly died, only so much worse in reality.

My guilt rises up as I see the thousands of Stefans before me, the young men who were killed, or wounded and lay bleeding. Had he called for me? Krysia had brought me here, I suspect, to give me some perspective and show me that life is fleeting. To help me move forward. But, instead, all of the reasons I cannot leave loom larger than ever.

"Such destruction," I lament, my words sounding tinny and inadequate.

"And not a drop of blood spilled on German soil," she remarks, gazing off into the distance. It is not meant as an insult; she is merely stating a fact. Picturing Stefan, I want to tell her that we had suffered, too. "There was enough stupidity on all sides, enough blame to go around," she adds as a concession, reading my thoughts. "But the victors will write history in their own way." I nod—laid out in the panorama before us is the reason the Allies will not be lenient, why the ideals embodied in Wilson's Fourteen Points will not be big enough to include the Germans. How can Georg not see that?

I'd been in the college library when one of the maids came to tell me about the armistice. A few days later, we assembled in the courtyard at Magdalen as the bell tolled, marking the official end to the war. We stood shoulder to shoulder—professors and students and porters and cooks, English and German alike. The war had changed so much—dukes and heirs had died alongside footmen and laborers. Women had worked as nurses and drivers and in the factories. Surely it all couldn't be put together the way it once was, an eggshell cracked in a thousand different pieces.

"The next war, I fear, will be even worse." Krysia's voice pulls me from my thoughts.

I turn to her in disbelief. "The next? Surely you don't think this will happen again."

"Not the men who fought this war, of course. The strongest pacifists are those who have seen battle. But governments have had a taste of the bloodshed and the power—and the weaponry will only get better."

My heart sinks as I realize she is right. They had called it the war to end all wars. But already there are whispers of newer, more sinister fears, gasses and other weapons that could take out the civilian populations of entire cities. Georg said militaries are needed in order to keep the peace.

If we cannot end war, then his work to prevent it, what he is trying to achieve, seems more important than ever.

"Some say if women could have voted, the war never would have started," I offer.

"Nonsense. Do you really believe those silly creatures who crow at the salons would have had any more sense than their husbands?" She is right. The war, more so than anything, had been about stupid pride, and the women, with their too-large hats and peacock feathers, had more than enough of that.

"At least one can speak openly of peace again," she remarks. I nod. Throughout the war it was considered treasonous and cowardly to speak of anything other than military victory. Only during the waning months did the word begin to creep into conversation again, a tacit recognition of the weariness and yearning for the end of the fighting that we had all secretly shared but not dared to voice. It was as if no one knew how to behave in peacetime again.

"Marcin wants to return to Krakow." She speaks into the air, not looking at me. "He can't compose here, he says, with all of the noise. He's begged me to come with him. But I can't leave Emilie." She has her own pain, I am reminded, of which she seldom speaks. I want to tell her to go with him, to leave the past behind. But who am I, childless and unable to escape my own past, to give her advice? I reach down and squeeze her hand gently.

"We should go," she says, as the sky begins to deepen at the edges.

"Thank you for bringing me."

"I've been meaning to come. And it can be helpful to

step out of one's own world, even for a bit, to gain some perspective." It's true. For a few hours, I've been able to escape all of my worries about the missing document, my questions of Georg and Stefan and the future. But as we wind through the hills and valleys, making our way back toward Paris, my heaviness grows once more.

"You're thinking about Georg." It is not a question and her voice sours as she says his name.

"You don't like him," I say to Krysia, dejected.

She shrugs. "I'm happy for you. It is good to see you wanting something—fighting for something—instead of letting life drag you along. But no, I don't like him. He's the enemy." There is a bitterness in her voice that I have never heard before.

"He's a German. Am I the enemy, too?" I feel again in that moment the gulfs of anger and hate that the war has sown, even in educated and worldly people such as she, pain too fresh for an armistice paper and a few months' passage of time to heal. "Don't you see, if we hate just because of where we come from, we're no better than the fools who started the war in the first place?"

She does not answer but continues driving. I gaze up at the sky, which is clear, but over the horizon to the west, dark gray clouds are forming. "Krysia, do you believe in fate?"

"You obviously do."

Suddenly it seems as though all my life I have been searching for the right answers, some hidden script I was supposed to follow without anyone actually giving it to me. Even my little rebellions, studying English instead of

Latin, music instead of art, had been well planned and de-signed in some way to show that my choices were the right ones. "I think there has to be some kind of order, a path."

But she shakes her head slightly. "I don't. We each have free will. There may be higher purpose, but the actual path each of us takes to get there, and whether we choose to accept it at all, is up to us." She turns to me. "If you can't let go of that fear of making the wrong decision, you will never be able to take the chances you must take to live life fully." She looks back at the road.

I consider this for the first time. I find romantic the no-tion that there is a purpose to it all, something that we are intended to do, a path—perhaps not unlike the people who preferred the firm constructs of the good old days. But as Krysia says—we each can choose our way. If it was all preordained and we stepped off, then what would hap-pen? "People make choices every day," I say, musing aloud. "Turn right or left…"

"Follow someone out of a party or not…" she chides.

I ignore the joke, nursing the more serious line of in-quiry. "And things would be very different if they did not."

"You have a choice. But you have to seize the moment or it may not come again. It is, as they say, now or never."

"But those choices have consequences," I counter, and with that she cannot argue. I could refuse to go back to Ber-lin, but so many people would be hurt—Stefan, for whom all hope would be lost, and Papa, too.

"I just want to go back to the way things were." But even as I speak the words I am not sure what I mean by them. Back to where? Life in Berlin with Stefan will never feel the same as it once has. London, our temporary stay among the enemy, was not the answer, either. I suppose I mean to some nameless place in time where it is just Papa and I with our books, but that place does not exist in a vacuum. There are others—Celia and Krysia and, yes, Georg.

"There is no back," she says gently. "We must forge on."

I nod. I've been a prisoner not of Papa's expectations or of Stefan, but of my own fears all of these years. "And speaking of forging on, what are you going to do about Ignatz?"

"I don't know." If I don't get the papers from Georg, Papa will be discredited. I am caught between the two men I care most about. "Talk to him, see if we can figure something out." I cannot keep running from Ignatz.

"I will take you to him." At the roundabout, she exits on a different road, heading to the northern edge of Paris. We reach the city limits and she continues in the direction of Montmartre, the motorcar engine struggling to ascend the steep hills. The neighborhood is ragtag, empty buildings and littered steps. "The artists used to live here before the center shifted to Montparnasse," she explains. She stops the car in front of a dilapidated building. "Stein lives on the first floor." I wait for her to offer to go with me but she does not.

The door to the apartment building is ajar so I enter and climb wood stairs so rickety I fear they will fall through. At the top, I knock. *"Da?"* Stein's voice calls and a moment later he throws open the door wearing only an undershirt and trousers. Behind him the flat is a cavernous space, open and bare, perhaps once an artist's studio. A woman I recognize from the bar sprawls in a chaise longue, clad in a dressing gown. I comprehend then just how far from my world I have come.

His bushy eyebrows pull together in a single scraggly line. "You! Do you have what I want?"

I swallow. "Not exactly. That is, I found it—it was a map and it showed markings at some of the eastern cities...." I falter, unable to convey the significance of what I had seen.

He rubs his hands together. "Perfect. Where is it?"

"I lost it. That is, I got the document but then it disappeared and..."

"Idiot!" Swift as a cat, he grabs me by the wrist and pulls me close. I cry out as great waves of pain shoot down my arm. I have never been struck, even lightly. Papa did not believe in spankings, despite admonitions from Uncle Walter and others that he would spoil me. It is the first time I have ever felt pain at the hands of another and I am frozen, unable to react. "Do you think I care about your excuses?" His breath is foul with vodka and smoke.

I pull away, stifling a cry at the burning of my skin as I wrest myself from his grasp. "How dare you?" I say, trying without success to keep the tremor from my voice. "I could have you arrested." I realize my mistake as soon as I have spoken. Threats will only feed his anger.

"Ignatz..." Before he can respond the woman from inside the apartment beckons.

"Three days," he hisses. "You have three days to get me what I want." He slams the apartment door, leaving me standing in the hallway, shaken.

I walk down the stairs and climb into the car. Krysia does not ask how it went and I do not offer. Instead, we drive silently into the night.

11

Papa is at his desk when I return, trying to read with the lamp turned down too low. That morning when I'd returned from Krysia's to wash and change, the apartment had been neater than I remembered leaving it, as if the maid had come on the wrong day. Now, it is a sea of strewn papers once more.

We eye each other warily. "I'm sorry," I say quickly, forgoing my usual stubbornness. I have no energy to argue after my day at the battlefields and confrontation with Ignatz.

Relief floods his face. He does not wish to continue our quarrel, either. "As am I. I just worry about you."

"I'm going to keep working for him, Papa," I say, struggling not to waver, to keep my voice clear and calm. I have never dared to defy my father like this and I can hardly believe my own resolve. Alienating him and leaving for good is unthinkable. But on this point I stand firm. "The work we are doing is important and it matters for the delegation and for the conference and for Germany."

His mustache pulls downward as he bites his lip, unable to disagree. "I understand, but I'm worried, *liebchen*. You seem to be attached to Captain Richwalder in a very strong way. This is not the time for complicated alliances," he adds, before I can protest. More so than fretting about propriety, Papa is concerned about me. He does not want me to get hurt. I should not be surprised—he has always put me first. But there is something more urgent about his worry this time, as if he is standing above me on a ladder, able to see things in a way that I can't.

"And then there is Stefan," he adds. "He's a good man and he cares for you deeply. He's sacrificed much." *I'm your daughter,* I want to say. *My happiness should be what matters.* But to say this would be to admit that my happiness lies with Georg, not Stefan, and how could I tell him that? "Your well-being is everything to me," Papa says, reading my thoughts. "I only wish…"

That the things that make me happy and the things that are good for me were one and the same. "I know." I raise my hand, warding off a return to the debate. "I went to Reims with Krysia today to see the battlefields."

He nods. "I saw your note that you'd gone somewhere."

"Do you mind?"

"To the contrary. I'm glad. I've been so busy with the conference, but it's no excuse. We've been remiss in not going and reminding ourselves of the very reason that we are here."

"I had no idea about the extent of the devastation. You had not told me."

"With Stefan fighting, I thought it might be too much. Sometimes I forget that you are not a child." He had been trying to shield my innocence. Still, I am frustrated by his hypocrisy—wanting me to be educated but not aware, teaching me to be curious and yet sheltering me from the truth.

"I was thinking of dinner in the city on Saturday, you, me and Celia," he says, changing the subject. There is a moment of uncomfortable silence between us. While I appreciate his need for her companionship, I have always resisted his attempts to bring Tante Celia closer into our circle. The last thing I want to do right now is sit down at a formal meal with the two of them. But he has conceded to my continuing work with Georg. And seeing the hope in his eyes, I cannot refuse. I smile. "Certainly, Papa."

Our conversation over, I walk to my room and change into my nightgown. Brushing my hair, I go to the window. It is raining now, thick round drops slapping against the window. My gaze travels down the street toward the hotel. I'd wanted to check on Georg, but the late hour, on top of Papa's forbidding me to go there, had stopped me. I undress and climb into bed, then lie awake in the darkness.

My thoughts roll back unexpectedly to the day Mother died. I came home from school that afternoon like any other. We'd been painting with watercolors and I'd done a scene of our garden I thought my mother might enjoy for her study. That the house was quiet was nothing new—she was often in her own quarters, napping or reading. I made myself a snack of cheese and crackers like I'd been taught, started on my homework. Twenty minutes passed, then thirty.

Finally the door to the kitchen opened but it was Papa who stepped through. This was not unusual, either—he sometimes worked in his home study. But his sleeves were rolled up and his hair disheveled in a way I never saw unless I caught him on the way to the water closet in the middle of the night. "Mama's gone," he said in a hoarse whisper and I thought he meant to the market or tea with a friend, though she had none of whom I knew. Seeing the faint red half circles around his lower eyelids like makeup in a play, I understood then that he meant dead. He had always tried to shield me from the worst, then as well as now.

A noise at the window pulls me from my memories. I push back the covers and as I walk to it, puzzled, the sound comes again, a pebble grazing the glass.

Georg stands on the pavement below, head tilted upward, face illuminated in the moonlight. "What are you doing here?" He does not answer. My stomach gives a little skip. But his standing on the street beneath my window is sure to attract attention. Suddenly I am mindful of my nightgown. "Can you wait a moment? I will be right down."

Quickly I dress and walk through the apartment to the front door. "Is someone here?" Papa calls from his desk.

Unable to bear the questions the truth would bring, I pretend not to hear him. Downstairs, I open the door. "Hello, Margot," Georg says, as though it were perfectly normal for us to meet like this. His eyes reflect like dark pools.

"Are you mad? You should be in bed." Behind him, raindrops lingering from the storm that has just ended fall from the eaves, the dripping sound rhythmic.

He shrugs. "I'm better now." I want to protest that he cannot possibly have recovered so quickly. His color is restored, though, and his face clear but for the faint half circles beneath his eyes. It is as if he has shrugged off serious illness like a bothersome cloak.

I've missed him, I realize, as a faint hint of his aftershave drifts beneath my nose. The past two nights apart have seemed so much longer. Then, remembering the missing document, I am flooded with panic. Perhaps he has noticed and that is why he is here.

"When you didn't come…" He falters. "I was worried."

I slump with relief, then hope he has not noticed. "I sent word." My note had only indicated I'd be gone the previous night, though, not tonight, as well. "I meant to return the papers today. I can get them right now if you need them."

"It isn't that. Rather, I wanted to know why you had not come."

Tante Celia appears behind him unexpectedly in the doorway. "Oh!" she says, mouth agape at the sight of the tall, handsome officer. I stare at her, equally surprised. Though I've long been aware of her slipping into the apartment to see Papa, this is the first time we've encountered each other at such a late hour of the night, when there is no respectable explanation for her appearance.

"Excuse me," Georg says, moving aside to let her in.

Celia steps around him, forgetting to leave her wet parasol outside. Then she turns to me. "Margot?" We stare at each other awkwardly.

"Tante Celia, may I introduce Captain Georg Richwalder? Georg, this is my…" I hesitate, considering a more explicit introduction, then decide against it. "This is my aunt."

He shifts his hat to his left arm and extends his right, kissing Tante Celia's hand as though we are at a ball and not the front door at a wholly improper hour of the night. "A pleasure."

Her eyes travel from him to me and there is a moment

of interminable silence, broken only by the drops falling from her umbrella to the marble floor. "I've heard so much about you," she says slowly. She could tell Georg about my engagement to Stefan. I hold my breath, waiting for the next drop to fall.

Upstairs Papa coughs. "I should go," she says, walking past us.

"I shouldn't be here unannounced at this hour," Georg frets when she has gone. "Only I saw these…" I notice then his hat is full of flowers, still wet from the storm. "Honeysuckle. You mentioned you like it and these are the first I've seen of the season. They've just begun to blossom," he adds, his eyes hopeful as a child's.

I step out of the apartment building and close the door behind me, then I reach for the flowers. They are a pretext, of course, an excuse to come and see me. At the bottom of the hat, my hand closes around something cool and metal. The flowers are held together by a finely linked bracelet of pearl, wrapped around the stems. "Oh, Georg. I couldn't possibly accept this."

"It's just a small token of my gratitude for your work, and for your kindness while I was ill. It was my mother's." He takes the bracelet from the flowers and fastens it around my wrist. "She believed that such things were to be worn, not shut away in a drawer from the light."

I open my mouth to protest. Such an elaborate gift isn't proper—I don't know him well enough. And it must hold a great deal of sentimental value for him, if he cared enough to bring it along with him to France. But the bracelet seems to forge to my skin as if a part of me and I cannot refuse it. He lifts my wrist to adjust the clasp. "What's this?" Illuminated in the glow of the streetlight is the scratch, red and swollen, from where Ignatz had grabbed me in threat. I am seized with the urge to tell Georg the truth about everything. There is a calm confidence about his demeanor that makes me want to trust him and I know he could fix this. But I cannot.

"I scraped myself earlier," I lie, cringing at the need to meet his concern with deception. Does he believe my explanation? Eager to distract him, I pull out a strand of honeysuckle from the bunch, inhaling the warm, fresh scent. Then I put the sprig in my hair, which is undone, combed long and full around my shoulders. "They're lovely. Thank you."

He nods formally, then takes his hat and turns to go. Behind him fireflies blink in the darkness.

"Wait." Setting the flowers on the table inside the doorway, I step out onto the street. The damp pavement releases its smells of earth and stone and waste.

He turns back, eyes hopeful. "Would you like to take a walk?"

"You shouldn't be walking anywhere in your condition."

"Nonsense. Come." I follow him down the dimly lit street. The air is more summer than spring now, any hint of a chill gone. Crickets chirp unseen and water trickles down the gutter along the roadside. "I love to walk at night," he adds.

I nod. I've often felt the pull from my open window to stroll the deserted streets and hear all of the noises so buried in the chaos of the day. I haven't done it, of course; for me alone, it wouldn't be safe. But walking beside Georg, I feel somehow protected. We pass a church and I peer up at figures carved in stone that stare down piously, demanding our repentance. The streets hold their breath, as if at any moment someone might step out and apprehend us.

We reach the park at the end of the street, the pavement fading into a dirt path that runs along a stream. Georg offers his arm and I hesitate. Then I reach out and wrap my hand around his thick forearm, the material of his uniform scratchy under my fingertips, skin warm beneath. We walk in silence for several minutes. The stream grows wider until it opens into a small lake with untended banks, flush with high curved reeds.

"Look." He points upward. I follow his hand, amazed at the bed of stars that unfurls above us. On the streets, the lights and tall buildings make it hard to see the sky properly. But in the shrouded darkness of the park nothing stands between us and them save a gentle canopy of branches and leaves. "Orion's Belt. The stars can be a kind of navigation tool when you are at sea. We have more modern equipment, of course, but in past centuries sailors navigated the world by the stars. As long as I could find Orion's Belt, I wasn't lost. The stars helped center me." There is a kind of hollowness to his voice, as though longing for such a centering now.

"I'm sorry I couldn't come to you these past two nights." I do not elaborate on my argument with Papa, knowing his misgivings would be hurtful to Georg. "I hope I haven't set you back too far in your work."

"I wasn't worried about that. I thought you were angry or upset." His voice trails off. He was concerned that I was put off by the things he said the other night. Despite his delirium, he remembers, and that makes his words real and impossible to deny. "You can stop working for me. The position I've put you in is untenable." My breath catches. Does he know somehow about Ignatz and the missing document, after all? For a moment, it is as if I am transparent, exposed. "I would understand if you didn't want to upset your father." I relax slightly. It is Papa's concerns he's picked up on intuitively. But I hate how that makes me sound like a child.

I consider what he has said. It had not occurred to me to stop working for him. I could even ask Papa to let me return to Berlin. It would solve many problems—Papa would no longer be angry and Ignatz, if he believed my termination involuntary, would have to accept that I could no longer help. But it would feel like giving up. And seeing Georg every day is the last thing I want to forgo.

No, I do not want to leave him. "Not at all," I say finally. "I won't give up on what we are doing."

His shoulders drop perceptibly with relief. "Good. I wanted to see you, too, because I have exciting news."

"Oh?"

"I received a new file from Berlin, one that had been lost in the archives—or so they thought. It belonged to a diplomat called Leimer, who had so many ideas similar to ours about how the German ground forces could partner with the West in peacetime. But then Germany signed the alliance with Russia and it was all moot. Leimer killed himself in protest."

"How awful!"

"Indeed, but his notes may have some suggestions about

how to combine the strengths of the two militaries that could be most helpful by analogy for our work."

"Have you gone through it yet?"

He shakes his head. "The file is massive and it only came late today." Yet he had broken from working on it to come find me. "I thought that perhaps if we divided it, we could get through it more quickly. Of course, the documents are already in German, but I thought that if we worked together it might go faster." Though, there was no need for translation, Georg was taking me into his confidence with the materials, treating me as his partner.

I think of the document I'd taken for Ignatz, seemingly disappeared. I do not know where it has gone, the extent of harm it might do in the wrong hands. Georg has not noticed it is missing, at least not yet. I look at him helplessly. I want to tell him everything. But I would have to admit what I had done and then he would despise me. And what could he do? Best to say nothing.

I shiver. Georg starts to remove his coat. I wave him off. "I'm not cold, thank you." My voice comes out more harshly than I intended. We are at a precipice, a place where one more step will make return impossible. I cannot bear to have him closer to me—even if it is only his coat.

"Oh…" He falters. "I'm sorry," he apologizes, mistaking my reticence for offense. Suddenly we are talking about something much larger than a coat. "If I said or did something…" He thinks I'm angry. The truth is just the opposite—it is my feelings and attraction to him that made me push him away.

Unable to bear the notion that I have hurt him, I reach out and touch his arm. "It's not that." Our eyes meet.

"Margot…" He lowers his head and suddenly his lips are lightly on mine, a question. I hesitate for a faint breath and then I am kissing him back, harder, swept away by things I had not dared to imagine. His hand cups my cheek. His mouth tastes of the sea and sand and faraway harbors, of longing and loneliness and loss, a wave pulling back from the shore, threatening to drag me along with it. Stefan has kissed me before but it was nothing like this….

Stefan. His face appears in my mind. I put my hand on Georg's chest, then pull away. "I can't." I struggle to catch my breath and right the world that wobbles around me. My cheeks burn. This is wrong. What kind of horrible woman am I, kissing another man while my husband lies wounded in a hospital bed? Georg's embrace holds everything I have ever needed, though I had not known until this very moment it existed. But it doesn't matter—I made a promise that I will honor. "I can't," I repeat.

His face crumbles. "I mistook your intentions and I apologize."

I reach for him. "Not at all. It's just that things are very complicated right now."

He pulls his arm from my grasp and steps away. "You needn't worry," he says. His voice is as stiff and formal as the day we met, all traces of the familiarity and closeness we've built up since then. "I understand now. You don't regard me in that way. It doesn't matter if it is about position or religion or something else. I accept it, and I won't bother you about it again…."

No, I want to shout. I have never cared about those so-cietal things and the notion that I do not like him, well, nothing could be further from the truth. But his logic makes sense—we are two young people and both, he thinks, single. There is no reason we could not be together if we chose. He smiles ruefully. "I should thank you. It has been a use-ful reminder of why I do not dabble in affairs of the heart." He turns abruptly. "I should see you home."

"Georg, wait…" I do not want to leave or to let go of this moment, the most real of my life. But he has already started from the water, back toward the garden path. I reach for him again. Suddenly the ground shifts beneath me. The bank. I've gone too close to the edge and the earth, softened by the recent rains, begins to give way. I fall backward as if in slow motion, my hands reaching toward Georg and closing around emptiness.

I sail through the air for what feels like several seconds before crashing into the water, icy as it engulfs me, seep-ing through my clothes. I flail my arms and try to kick, but my legs become tangled amid my skirt. The water begins to close over my head.

Georg is beside me then, pulling me to the surface, one arm around my neck and the other my waist as he guides me to shore. "Are you all right?"

"Quite." I tremble, as much from my terror at encoun-tering the water as from the night air, frigid against my wet skin. "I told you I wasn't much of a swimmer."

He laughs as we reach the bank. "That's an understate-ment. The water is hardly deeper than you are tall, though panic can make things seem much worse." Then his expression grows serious. "You're soaked," he says, apparently heedless that he is wet, as well. He wraps me in his coat and this time I do not protest. "We need to get you back to the hotel."

I stand, holding my soaked skirt aloft so as not to trip. "I'm fine." But I am unable to stop my teeth from chattering. "I'll just head home."

"Come back to the hotel and while your things are drying out, I can show you the Leimer file."

"Fine," I relent, my curiosity about the new documents piqued. It would be better, too, to avoid seeing Papa and Celia like this and facing their questions.

Ten minutes later, we reach the hotel and he leads me up the back stairs to avoid the lobby. Inside, I wait uncertainly in his sitting room until he reappears, producing a soft, gray dressing gown. "Put this on." I walk to the water closet and come out a few minutes later, his oversize robe swimming around me. He takes my dress from me and hangs it by the fire he's started. "This should dry in no time."

He looks toward the desk, piled high with his papers, and I expect him to pull out the file. But instead he hands me a cup of tea. "Sit." I hesitate. Talking to him in such a state is ridiculously awkward and improper. But there is something strangely delicious about being swallowed by his oversize robe, the familiar smell of his aftershave wafting up from the collar. I wanted to come here tonight, I realize, and it had nothing to do with the new documents or avoiding Papa. I draw my knees up close beneath me as he adds wood to the fire.

He stands and walks into the bedroom once more, then

returns a moment later with a small tube. "Let me see your wrist," he says firmly, kneeling in front of me. He squeezes some salve from the tube and rubs it into the wound where Ignatz had grabbed me, the warm pleasure of his touch mixing with dull pain, stirring something deep inside me.

Finally, he sits across from me, then stares into the fire, not speaking. Is he thinking about our kiss, or the fact that I pushed him away? I stop, flooded by regret, feeling Georg's lips so full on mine. The kiss was like nothing I have ever experienced. Live for the moment, Krysia would have admonished. It was all any of us had anymore. But I had turned away, letting as ever all of my self-doubts ruin the kiss. Surely there would not be another.

I notice for the first time the sword that is on the mantelpiece. A shiver runs through me. "They permitted us to keep our weapons," he says. "I do not, of course, carry mine here."

"Have you ever used your sword?"

"Technically, it's a saber." Though his tone is not unkind, I am embarrassed, as though I should have known. "No." His jaw sets grimly. "I haven't used it, but the destruction I've caused is no less egregious. I hate war."

"But you're still in the navy. Isn't that something of a contradiction?"

He shakes his head. "I'm a sailor and I can't abandon that. And I'm proud to serve Germany, even now. I believe that a military, properly designed, can be a deterring force, a valuable part of international relations and peace."

We sit in silence for a few minutes. We should be working. There is much to be done. I realize then that I am not just helping Georg. It has become my mission, too. "You mentioned the Leimer file?"

"Oh, yes," he said, as if while we were talking, he had forgotten. He goes to the desk once more and pulls out a file several inches thick. "They don't appear to be in any particular order," he notes, dividing the stack in two and handing half to me. I begin to page through the materials, noting on a separate paper a few pages of interest. We work alongside each other in silence.

"Your dress should be dry," he concedes some time after midnight, an unmistakable note of reluctance to his voice. "Perhaps if you'd like to take some of the documents, you can review them while I'm meeting with the delegation tomorrow."

"Certainly," I reply, marveling at the ease with which he gives me access to the material. How can I possibly betray him again?

"Is something wrong? You look so sad."

"I'm fine," I say, searching for a plausible explanation. "I just get a bit lost sometimes."

He reaches over and I freeze. Will he try to kiss me again? But he just brushes a smudge of dirt from beneath my right eye, the edge of his finger grazing the lashes before pulling away.

I carry my dress into Georg's room and loosen the robe. I pause, standing unclothed in the center of his room, seized with the urge to lie down in his bed, just inches away. "Margot?" he calls from the sitting room. Hurriedly, I put on the dress. The material is a bit scratchy from the quick drying and a faint pond smell lingers.

I step back out into the sitting room. "I should get home before Papa begins to worry." His brow furrows.

"Does he mind your being out with me?" His question asks something deeper: Does Papa know of the feelings that have transpired between us?

"I don't know." A frown flickers across Georg's face, disappointment, perhaps, that I have not been more forthright with Papa about what is transpiring between us. But how could I have possibly? It's been mere days and whatever has grown between us is too fledgling and strange to understand myself, much less explain. Even without Stefan and the other complications, I could not have told him. "That is, he's been so busy. I haven't had the chance to speak with him about things." It is a lie, I think, remembering our fight about Georg and our conversation just hours ago.

But Georg holds up his arm, warding off my excuses. "Of course not. No explanation needed. How silly of me to have thought… Your father would want someone Jewish, and a learned man to be sure."

"It's not that," I protest quickly. "I would never care about such matters, if things were right."

"If things were right," he repeated slowly, eyes meeting mine with more hope than I have ever seen. Guilt rises. I am leading him on and I cannot stop myself. His face brightens. "I never should have expected you to tell him. You go home now. I should not have had you come here like this. First thing tomorrow I will see your father and ask his permission to call on you formally."

Panic floods my brain. If Georg goes to Papa, he will learn the truth about everything. "Georg, no." He blanches with apprehension that all of his original concerns of not being good enough to be accepted are in fact true. "Papa's just so preoccupied with the conference work right now. It is taxing his health, which is already in a dreadful state." I curse myself for using Papa's heart condition as an alibi. "If we just wait until after the plenary session next week, we can have you around for dinner and then you can ask." I cringe inwardly at the lie. It will never be okay for Georg to ask Papa to court me. But at least this will buy me some time.

"Fine," he says, somewhat mollified.

"I should go," I say again, picking up the documents.

"I'll walk you home."

"Really, that isn't necessary." I am not keen to be seen with him at this hour and my excuses will be so much easier to make if I can be caught alone.

He raises his hand, unwilling to be dissuaded. Neither of us speaks on the short walk down the street to our apartment building. He stops a few meters from the doorway, a concession to the secret I've asked him to keep for now. There is a moment of silence that seems eternal. Our eyes meet uncertainly. Will he try to kiss me again?

But he nods and tips his hat formally, grasping the present limitations—a tactical retreat. There is a moment of awkward hesitation as we watch one another uncertainly. "We'll resume work tomorrow, then?" For everything that has transpired between us, there is still the work.

"Good night," I manage, my voice barely a whisper. Everything has changed between us in a way that cannot be undone. I turn and walk into the apartment building without looking back, feeling his eyes on me.

12

The next night when I walk into the hotel library, it is dark and empty, with a stale smell that suggests Georg has not yet been there this evening.

Carrying the documents I've brought back with me, I walk down the hall and knock on the door to his room. "Hello?" There is no answer. I turn the handle and push open the door. But his rooms are still, as well. Six forty-five, the clock on the wall reads. He must be in meetings with the delegation. I had not planned to come early, but since I have…my eyes travel across the room to the desk and the pile of papers I'd searched the night he was ill. Perhaps if I look again, I can find another report that details the information Ignatz wants. Of course, it is risky—Georg could return at any second. But time is running out and there's no reason to believe I will have another chance to search the apartment alone. I have to try.

I move toward the desk, peering over my shoulder. Then I lift the stack to the midpoint, separating it close to where I found the original map. There are cables, but they reference other matters, seemingly unrelated to military installations in the east. I page deeper.

The door creaks suddenly. I jump back and the documents scatter like falling leaves. "Georg," I manage, as I kneel hurriedly to pick them up. "You startled me. I was early," I add. I'm babbling now. "I came in here looking for the rest of the Leimer file."

He bends and takes the documents I've collected from me in one fell swoop, then sets them back on the desk. "It's in the library." I follow him down the hall. He does not sound suspicious or annoyed. But when we reach the library, his brow is furrowed, bottom lip drawn in consternation. He looks tired and there are dark circles under his eyes. Perhaps the strain of our walk the previous night was too much.

"What is it?" I ask, putting my hand on his forearm instinctively.

"A document is missing." My breath catches. Easy, I think. There are thousands of documents. It could be something else. "A map of weapons depots to the east." Now I cease breathing entirely. "I received a call from the delegation saying that they needed that document and when I went to fetch it from the file, it was gone."

My pulse quickens. The very paper I had stolen was the one that they sought. What are the odds? It is almost as if someone knew. But how is that possible? "Don't worry," he soothes, seeing my distress. "It wasn't in the binder you took, or even the ones you've reviewed here." No, it is from the pile I riffled while you were semiconscious with fever. "But it's terribly disturbing."

"Perhaps it was a mistake and it was missing before you came to Paris?"

"I'm afraid not. All of the documents were meticulously catalogued." Georg was far too orderly to leave such things to chance. "And I've seen this particular one since coming here. It is definitely missing." He drops into a chair. "And that is disastrous."

"Surely they won't think you lost it intentionally."

He jumps up again. "Perhaps not. But it could cause problems. You see, there are deep factions within the delegation." I nod. Papa had alluded to as much. "As with any political group, there are different views. The hardliners—mostly the older members—feel that there is no reconciliation with the West, that even in defeat we should hold our ground and remain an island." He is pacing now, one hand at the back of his neck. "They regard my views of possible collaboration on future military endeavors as too liberal. The only reason they tolerate me at all is because of my military service record. And if they think I've lost a document, perhaps even on purpose, it will seriously undermine the credibility of my position and my work will be jeopardized."

Suddenly my violation of his trust seems more egregious than ever. "There has to be something that we can do to mitigate the damage."

"It's more than that, actually. The document did not just contain the German information. I have an ally, you see." I cock my head. "In the ministry is a young French lieutenant, partially of Russian descent. I had the opportunity to make acquaintance with the officer several years ago before the war on a joint training exercise and we stayed in touch. Lieutenant Bouvier believes, as I do, in the future of joint cooperation. So we've been, *ahem,* sharing information where it could be beneficial to that cause."

"I see." Georg has a contact inside the French foreign ministry. I had no idea. All of this time I've been so preoccupied with my own secrets, it never occurred to me that he might have one or two of his own.

"I'm so sorry I didn't tell you, Margot. At first, I didn't know you all that well. It's one thing to tell you about my work, but to jeopardize someone else is another matter. And then it didn't seem to matter as much."

"It's fine." I am hardly in a position to be holding grudges over secrets.

"I need to get word to Lieutenant Bouvier that our information has been compromised. But it hasn't been safe for us to talk for months, and I don't dare call the ministry or go there for fear of attracting attention."

"I can do it," I blurt without thinking. "That is, I can deliver a message to Lieutenant Bouvier for you."

"Margot, no. I couldn't ask." But I can see his mind working, the solution forming even as he protests it.

"I'm familiar with the ministry." It is perhaps an overstatement, but I was inside a handful of times with Papa when we stayed in Paris. And no one is likely to question a young woman such as myself who might easily be a courier. "Write the note," I instruct, with more force than I thought I would have dared.

The next morning at nine, I step out of the taxi in front of the foreign ministry. I cross the street quickly, fighting the urge to run and attract attention as I make my way to the entrance at the side of the massive building. Time is of the essence, Georg had said the previous evening, and I would have gone then and there, had the late hour not made it impossible. Instead, I had lain awake most of the night, plotting how I could get to Lieutenant Bouvier. At the gate, I stop, steeling myself. The arched entranceway is a swirl of bodies, diplomats arriving, couriers setting out on errands, visitors claiming appointments and waiting to be seen. I weave through the horde authoritatively. I do not stop at the gate, but wave airily the visitor badge I'd found in our apartment, hoping that the guard will not notice from this distance that it expired months ago.

Inside, the West Entrance Hall is quiet by contrast, just a few groups of suited men clustered on the red velvet couches talking. My heels echo conspicuously as I cross the marble floor.

"Mademoiselle?" a voice says behind me as I reach the base of the wide staircase.

I freeze and turn back, certain that I have been caught. *"Oui?"*

Standing before me is a uniformed guard who cannot be more than eighteen or so himself. "You look lost. Can I help?"

"I'm trying to find my father, Professor Rosenthal, who is an advisor to the conference."

"I believe they're presently in the salon on the second floor." I continue two flights up the staircase. When I reach the landing, I start down the high-ceilinged corridor, which is lined with framed tapestries. Thick velvet curtains, held back with gold brocade, frame the windows.

At the end of the hall, I find a narrower, back stairway. Looking over my shoulder, I walk down to the floor below. Away from the ceremonial halls, the decor is less ornate:

there is a row of simple oak doors with brass nameplates beside them, modest lighting instead of chandeliers. Following the instructions Georg had given me, I reach a door marked "E. Bouvier" and knock.

"Oui?" a female voice calls. I push the door open. Inside, a woman in a navy skirt and blouse sits behind a desk.

"I'm looking for Lieutenant Bouvier."

"That's me."

I falter. I had never considered that Lieutenant Bouvier might be a woman. She is beautiful with a short tight cap of black curls and bright blue eyes. "I'm sorry, I had not expected…"

"A woman?" She smiles wearily. "I was in the nursing corps. Lieutenant was my military title." Taking in her button nose and perfect lips, which form a pout without the help of makeup, I am flooded with jealousy. How well does she know Georg? Had they been involved? "Can I help?" she prompts.

"Captain Richwalder sent me," I say.

"Georg?" A flash of intimacy crosses her face, confirming everything I feared about the two of them. "I haven't seen him in years."

"He wanted me to give you this." I hold out the note. She unfolds it and as she reads, her eyes widen with alarm. Then she crumples the note in her fist. "Thank you."

"He wanted you to know so that he could offset any damage from the loss," I say, eager to show her that I am not just a messenger but a partner in Georg's work. An idea begins to form. "Georg mentioned that you might have a copy of the map that was lost."

Her eyes narrow. "Did he want it?"

I nod. "A mimeograph, yes." I hold my breath, waiting for her to ask why he had not requested the copy in his note. But she turns and disappears through another door. My heart begins to pound. If I can get her to give me a copy of the map, I can pass it on to Ignatz as I had originally intended.

Several minutes later, she returns carrying a piece of paper and starts to hand it to me. Then she hesitates, leaving my hand outstretched midair. "Be careful with this. Many—including Georg—could be hurt if it falls into the wrong hands."

I swallow as she seems to see right through me. "I shall." Outside the office, I pause, shaking. Then I walk down the hallway to the wide marble staircase, folding the paper as I walk.

As I round the bend, Papa appears several steps below. "There you are." Hurriedly, I jam the paper into my bag. "The guard rang that you were here and asking for me, but you never appeared. Margot, what is it? Are you ill?"

"Not at all." I search for an explanation. "I was in the city and I wanted to check if you were free for coffee."

He studies me, not quite believing the lie. I meet his eyes, willing him not to look down and notice the paper sticking out of my half-open bag. The realization that I had come on an errand for Georg and had become so involved in his work would surely be the final straw. "I'm afraid I can't," Papa says. "Do you mind?"

"Not at all. I'll go visit Krysia instead." I kiss him on

the cheek and continue past him on the stairs, warding off further discussion.

Outside, I walk to the bank of the Seine, eager to get as far from the ministry as possible. I start along the quay, trembling. I had done it, delivered Georg's message and even gotten the document I need for Ignatz. I pull it from my bag, holding it tightly against the sharp breeze that comes off the water. I study the map, an exact duplicate of the one I had lost. I can give it to Ignatz right now and be done with this once and for all. I gaze across the river toward the Eiffel Tower, remembering the pain as Ignatz grabbed my wrist. Once he has the map, I will be free.

Two hours later, I return to Versailles and enter the hotel. I knock on the door to the conference room across the hall from the library where the German delegation meets. "Captain Richwalder, please," I say to the aide. A moment later, Georg appears. "Margot, what are you doing here?" he asks, closing the door behind him.

I peer over my shoulder to make sure no one is listening. "I got through to your contact," I say, deliberately omitting her name. Relief crosses his face. "And here." I pass him the document. His eyes widen. Having the map will solve many problems for him. I had walked the riverbank for nearly an hour, trying to figure out what to do and to work up the nerve to give the map to Ignatz. But in the end, I could not bring myself to surrender it to him. For even as I had stood on the quay, seeing his glowering eyes, Georg's trusting face had appeared above his. The document that could have satisfied Ignatz would also save Georg. I could not take it from him.

Seeing his gratitude and relief now, I know that I made the right choice. "Margot, I cannot thank you enough."

"Lieutenant Bouvier is a woman," I remark, hating the jealousy in my own voice. "You had not mentioned."

He looks up from the paper. "Does that matter?"

"Not at all," I reply quickly. "She's quite beautiful, though."

"I suppose, though I really had not noticed." The explanation sounds implausible, but his voice is sincere. "It's funny, isn't it, how we feel that way about some people and not others?" I do not answer. Behind him a door opens and an older man peers out expectantly. "I must return to the meeting."

"Of course."

As I turn away, he clasps my forearm. I freeze, caught off guard by the unexpected touch, the warmth of his fingers against my skin. "Margot, wait…" He looks down, as if he has surprised himself. But he does not let go. Several seconds of silence pass between us. "Let me show you my appreciation. Dinner in Paris, tonight? I'll get a pass and the car and we'll have a nice meal. No talk about work or the conference or the treaty, I promise."

I hesitate. *Walk away,* a voice inside me says. The kiss last night, spontaneous and unplanned, seems somehow less culpable than a planned deception. "How can we possibly spare a night of work?"

He considers the question, torn between wanting to take

me out and needing to press forward. "Dinner first, then we can come back and work late."

My stomach flutters. "That would be fine," I say in spite of myself.

"You'll go out with me, then, a proper date?" He repeats the question, not quite believing my response the first time.

"Yes." I shouldn't, but I will.

His face brightens, hopeful as a boy's. "Shall I pick you up at seven?"

An older man appears behind him suddenly in the door frame then. "Captain Richwalder, I apologize, but we really must…" He stops midsentence, noticing Georg's hand on my arm.

But Georg does not pull away, and in that moment, everything between us is out in daylight, exposed. The man clears his throat and disappears back into the room.

"Tonight, then," Georg whispers. Then he steps away and closes the door between us, leaving me alone in the hallway, shaking.

13

⁓⟞━━━━━━━━━⟞⁓

That night at seven I stand before the mirror putting the final touches on my outfit, a dress of simple blue satin, adorned only by my mother's necklace and the bracelet Georg had given me. I study my reflection, fretting. Georg had remarked once that he disliked the stiffer, more ruffled fashions, but perhaps my choice is too plain for a Saturday evening in Paris. If only I had something a bit more womanly to wear, or perhaps some more of the things Celia always tried to press on me, such as a pencil to darken my brows or a bit of rouge.

The doorbell rings and I press the buzzer. "Come in," I say when Georg reaches the landing. He wears the same dress uniform as the night of the dinner party, epaulets at the shoulder, three gold bands around the jacket forearms.

But he stands awkwardly inside the doorway. Though we have been alone any number of times at the hotel, it is somehow different here and he is reluctant to enter. "Your father isn't here," he observes. I cannot tell if he is disappointed or relieved.

I notice an envelope lying on the table by the door. It is a letter I received earlier from Stefan and I had opened it hurriedly, barely scanning the scrawl. It sits now just inches from where Georg stands, the photograph Stefan had included facing upward on top. I hold my breath, waiting for Georg to ask about the man in the picture, to come to the realizations I will not be able to deny. A brother, I imagine claiming, if he asks. A cousin. Then I stop, mortified. How far will my lies go?

But he does not look down, instead staring only at me. "Shall we?" I ask. He clears his throat, nods.

The sky is still bright forty-five minutes later, as the car winds its way into Paris, the late-day sun lingering like the patrons drinking coffee at the sidewalk cafés. Georg stares out the window eagerly in spite of the disinterest he'd professed when we first spoke. He has only been into the city once since arriving, I realize, and that was the night he collapsed at the dinner. The car pulls to a stop by the river, just beneath the Louvre. "Do you feel like walking for a bit?" Georg asks after he had come around to offer me his arm. There is an air of formality about him not present the other times we've been together.

We stroll along the quay, past the slanted carts where merchants sell used books and other wares. The waters of the Seine high and brackish. At the base of a bridge, a group of small children hide, pretending to shoot one another with imaginary guns. Georg shakes his head. "How can they still play at war after all that has happened?"

A few minutes later we turn from the river and climb toward the Champs-Élysées. As we pass one of the hotels, lively music seeps out through the open window. Inside, couples glide elegantly across the floor. The Saturday night dances have become something of an institution in the city, persisting even through the darkest days of the war. I've always been curious about the waltzes and other more modern steps, the way that the couples move so easily in tandem. I imagine then Georg taking me in his arms and leading me across the floor. "Not much of a dancer, I'm afraid," he says, noticing my interest.

"Me, either," I reply quickly, wanting to put him at ease. It is not just the dancing that is off-putting to him. The parties are sponsored by the British and he would not be welcome there.

We continue, navigating the sidewalks crowded with other pedestrians enjoying the summer evening stroll. Several women in fashionable dresses give Georg sidelong looks, but he does not seem to notice. A few minutes later, he stops before Maxim's. "I thought we'd eat here," he says. It is a mistake, I decide instantly as we pass beneath the red-and-gold awning through the double oak doors. Georg has not spent enough time in the city to realize that the once-elegant restaurant has changed since the deluge of foreigners arrived. But I do not want to hurt his feelings.

Inside, the front room is packed thick. A group of American officers stands by one of the high tables, enjoying a champagne dinner, great quantities of alcohol and not much else. They are bantering loudly with two women at the bar, who with their heavy makeup and skimpy outfits make no effort to conceal the fact that they are prostitutes. Through another doorway, dance music blares and bodies press together, twirling as gaily as though it were midnight. Something is different from the few other times I've been. Though the conference continues apace, there is a sense of it all ending. In days or weeks, the treaty will be announced and then the conference will be over. There is an intensity to the revelers, as though they need to drink it all in before it is gone.

"Perhaps somewhere quieter," Georg frets as we squeeze between tables in the bar, inching toward the restaurant seating. "One of my colleagues recommended it, only..."

"It's fine," I reassure. He has put much thought into the evening and I don't want to disappoint him.

He wrinkles his nose as a plume of smoke drifts up from one of the tables. "Does it bother you?" I ask.

"Living in such tight quarters on the ship, I inhaled enough of others' smoke for a lifetime." He raises his voice slightly to be heard above the din. "Not a major matter. But it's funny, isn't it, the way that living somewhere else can change you? For example, the officers' quarters on the ship were quite nice, but the food ran scarce and once when we were stranded and unable to make it in to port the only thing we had to eat for two weeks were turnips. I've not been able to swallow one since."

I laugh knowingly. Living abroad had changed me, too, not as profoundly as the war had Georg, but in a dozen more subtle ways. Across the room, the banter has picked up, the soldiers now openly catcalling to the women at the bar. Georg scowls. "This is most improper. I'm so sorry."

"Not at all."

Georg takes my arm without asking and draws me close. As he scans above the crowd for the maître d', a large-bellied man jostles into him. "Excuse me," Georg says reflexively, though the fault is not at all is.

"No excuse, you peacock. Your uniform," the man jeers drunkenly. "It is a relic." I picture then the stares Georg attracted on the street. Perhaps it was not admiration at all, but anger at his audacity for openly identifying himself as a German soldier.

"We are at peace, sir," Georg responds stiffly, his cheeks flushing as though he has been slapped.

"It is still an offense," the man retorts. Georg winces. To him, the uniform is second skin, the only thing he has known. What future has he without it? He cannot—will not—deny who he is to appease the social and political sensibilities of the day. Without provocation, the man spits in Georg's direction. I can feel Georg's arm tightening in anger and I press on it, willing him not to respond, and pull him toward the exit.

"I'm sorry that you had to see that," he says when we've reached the street, wiping the spittle from his lapel.

"Does it happen often?"

"Quite, I'm afraid."

"Have you ever thought about not wearing the uniform?"

"To avoid trouble, you mean?" I nod. "I considered it in the beginning. But I'm an officer of the German navy. It is a question of honor."

Honor. Everything Georg does is about honor. Not stubbornness, but something born of a deeper, more principled place. And me? I've lied to him about Stefan, deceived him by taking the document. No, I'm the furthest thing from honorable. "I'm sorry," he says again.

"Perhaps we should just return to Versailles." His eyes

betray his disappointment as he looks out across the river where a ribbon of pink sky sits atop the roofs like icing on a cake.

I shake my head, set upon saving our evening in Paris. "I have an idea. Come." It is my turn to lead now, taking his hand and retracing the route toward the nearby neighborhood where our hotel had been. I stop in front of a crémerie. "Wait here." A few minutes later I emerge with a basket. "We're not done," I say playfully, and dutifully he follows me farther down the road to the bike shop I frequented when we lived here. I pay the shopkeeper for the bicycle rentals and wheel them out onto the pavement.

"Bicycle riding?" he asks in disbelief as I push one in his direction. "That hardly seems…"

I fasten the basket to the handlebars. "You don't ride?"

"Well, perhaps a few times as a boy. And horses, of course."

"It's not that different." Then I stop. He seems so well and happy now, it is easy to forget that just a few days earlier he had been gravely ill. "Perhaps the strain will be too much."

"I'm fine." He squares his shoulders, rising to the challenge.

I mount my bike. "Then catch me if you can." I navigate carefully down the street in the direction of the park.

"Margot…" Georg's voice has grown fainter as he falls behind in the distance. I glance over my shoulder, smiling at the sight of him wobbling uncertainly on his bike, shaky as a newborn calf. When we reach the entrance to the park,

I pedal faster. I've not ridden since our move to Versailles and I savor the familiar burning in my legs.

Georg is beside me then, grabbing the handlebar of my bike to slow me. "Mercy!" He laughs and topples his bike sideways to the grass, falling with mock dramatics, more playful than I've ever seen him.

Reluctantly, I set mine down beside him. "We'd best pull farther off the path, so we're not made to leave at dusk." We turn the bikes into a clearing set apart by tall bushes. Suddenly it feels as though we are miles away from the city.

"That's better," he says. He means the two of us alone, freed from the congestion of the restaurant and the streets. Alone together is the only place this seems to work. "Though we should have a blanket." He frowns. "Your dress will get soiled."

I run my hand along the soft, dry patch of moss beneath us. "Nonsense." I pull from the basket the food I purchased. "Just an assortment of cheese and some pâté. I hope you like them."

"I'll eat anything as long as it's not pickled. I had enough of the canned and the salted on the ship to last me a life-time."

"And turnips," I tease, "don't forget those." Hungry after the bike ride, I spread some chèvre, thick and salted, on a piece of baguette and take a bite. As I chew, I peer through the trees. Though I cannot see it from here, I know that just on the other side of the brush sits the pond where I saw Krysia watching the children that first day.

"What?" I am suddenly aware of George's eyes upon me.

"You eat with such gusto," he remarks, and I can feel

myself blush. My failure to be ladylike coming back yet again to haunt me. "I mean that as a good thing. You just seem to grab life and shake it like a tree, finding all that falls from it."

I laugh and for a moment it is as if we are any other young couple, in love and carefree, shed of all the secrets and unspoken things that stand between us and the future. "So have you had the chance to look through any more of the Leimer file?" I ask as I pull the bottle of chardonnay from the basket and hand it to him to uncork.

"I went through it last night," he replies as he deftly inserts the corkscrew and turns.

"I left so late it must have been this morning, really."

"Perhaps. Anyway, it's fascinating. Leimer's ideas about how to synchronize the strengths of the various militaries could be very useful and…" He breaks midsentence and smiles sheepishly. "I promised not to talk about work tonight."

"I don't mind," I reply. It is the truth. Work is so much a part of who we are together. *We.* "I'm the one who brought it up."

I lift a glass for him to fill. But when I raise the second glass, Georg shakes his head. "I've decided to stop drinking for a time."

It must be a very recent decision, I think, remembering the wine on his breath a few nights earlier. "Because of your illness?"

"Because of a lot of things. It just gets too easy at sea— beer when the water is fetid, wine with dinner, brandy after." Though his tone remains even, there is a scratch to the underside, like a phonograph record played too many times. "The evening before the battle was something of a celebration." Though he does not specify, I know he means Jutland. There is a care to his voice, a thoughtfulness to the way he forms the words, that tells me he has not shared this story before. "There had been word of a victory, which was becoming increasingly rare. We'd opened the last of the meat stores and the better champagne. I drank more than usual and had retired. If I hadn't I might have heeded the warning signs, seen the way the British ships were amassing. By the time I'd awoken, the *Pommern* had already been hit." He blames himself for not being able to stop the battle that had taken his brother's life.

"Georg, there was nothing you could have done. Even if you'd sensed it…"

But he shakes his head, unwilling to accept any account that does not accord with the narrative he has told himself for so long. "Perhaps I could have signaled for some reinforcements or perhaps repositioned the fleet." What is it about ourselves that makes us believe we can change great events with our thoughts and deeds? It feels a kind of hubris. "And then they made me into some kind of hero. I protested, tried to tell them the truth, but they said it was needed for the morale of the men. It was a lie."

It was the dishonesty, perhaps more so than anything else, that Georg found impossible to bear. I understand so much more about him now, his solitary nature, the way part of him always seems to be elsewhere. What would he say if he knew the truth about me and the things I have done?

He looks up as though he has forgotten I was there. "You must think me a terrible coward."

"Not at all." I reach out and take his hand, not caring now about the propriety as I try to wash away his self-loathing. It takes courage, I want to tell him, to speak the truth. I am the coward here.

"I'd like to leave," Georg says. For a minute, thinking he means our date, I am hurt. Did I say something to offend him? "Head south perhaps, to the Mediterranean." He is referring to the conference and the city. But he seems so intent and driven by the work he is doing here. I nod, recognizing his desire to flee the stifling confines of the city. "Let's do it," he says. "There are places, you know, located by the mountains as well as the sea. Places we could both love." He's serious.

"Georg, what about the conference? And your work?" And my father and my husband and a dozen other reasons I cannot say.

"Perhaps when the conference is over and we are both back in Germany..." he begins, trying again. I do not respond. Berlin means Stefan and the future that inevitably awaits me, the end of all of this. Then he breaks off. "Of course, I'm not presuming that you would want to be with me." He has mistaken my hesitation for demurral. I take his hand, uncertain what to say. Paris is something of a vacuum, so many people brought together in this odd little whirlwind where none of the rules apply. Back home life is stratified, divided, and Georg and I come from different worlds, religions, politically and socially. Even without Stefan, our lives in Germany would be so disparate. But I would transcend all of that for the chance to be with him. Could every day be exactly like this, glorious and sparkling? An image comes into my mind then of Georg as an old man, sharing a cup of tea in our parlor, long after the children have grown and left. I stop, struck by the vision. It is so different from the life I usually envision for myself and yet in that moment I know it is exactly what I want. We could be this good every single day, waking up side by side laughing and talking.

"Margot," he says, squeezing my hand. "We can be together. Why do you resist?" He does not know, as I do, that our days are numbered, that each passing night brings us closer to the fated end.

What will you do after the war? Krysia's words echo in my mind. The answer is so different now. I'm not just running *from* Stefan but *to* Georg and yet at the same time there's an inevitability to the fact that it must end. Is that what makes it so good, the knowledge that these few moments we have together are stolen? No, I decide, looking across at Georg. There's a connection between us, a spark that would burn through the decades, through the everyday, and all of the great hurts and triumphs. I imagine a child then, a boy, with Georg's strong features. My stomach jumps.

"Shh." I lean in, desperate to silence the questions, to stop my head from whirling like a carousel. This time I kiss him, my lips mashing clumsily against his. I wait for him to pull away and tell me it isn't proper. But he presses into me, meeting the intensity of my mouth, probing, upping the stakes. The voices of wrong and right fade in my mind, drowned out by a low moan that sounds foreign escaping my lips as he presses me back toward the ground.

From the far side of the bushes comes a loud noise, an explosion tearing us abruptly apart. "What on earth?" Georg leaps to his feet, reaching for his waist and the weapon that is not there.

The noise comes again, a succession of popping sounds. "It's all right," I soothe, standing hurriedly. But he remains in front of me as we step from the grove onto the path, arm around me protectively.

Fireworks begin to erupt in the distance behind the Eiffel Tower. "Oh!" I exclaim, and we stop to admire the spectacle as great dazzling bursts of green and red and blue fire light up the night sky.

"But why?" he asks, more puzzled than delighted. He has a point—there is no holiday or other reason for them. "Something has happened. We should go." I repack the basket hurriedly and start toward the bicycle shop. When we've returned the bikes, we walk in the direction of the river. The fireworks display has ended then, the sky cloudy with their dust. The faint smell of gunpowder hangs in the air. The streets are crowded, as nearly filled with people as the day Wilson arrived, buzzing excitedly.

Georg takes his hand and mine and places them in my pocket for warmth. He stops unexpectedly and turns to me and his lips are upon mine then and suddenly it is as if the crowds around us have disappeared. "I'm sorry. But I had to do that one last time, before…"

"I understand." Before the fireworks and whatever lay beyond them change our world forever.

He takes my hand once more and leads me in the direction of a newsstand, hands the boy a few coins for a paper, which gives off the smell of fresh ink. "It's the treaty," he says, scanning the headline. "The terms have been announced." As he reads, his eyes widen with disbelief. I lean in over his shoulder. Millions of marks in reparations, the German military to be disbanded immediately.

"This is not peace," he says, struggling to maintain his composure. "This is a crucifixion. I must get back to Versailles at once."

"Yes, of course." I cannot help but be disappointed at our evening ending so abruptly.

Holding tightly to my arm, Georg cuts a path through the crowd. "Across the river," he says, pulling me toward the bridge. On the other side, he hails a taxi, handing the driver several bills once we are inside. "Versailles, immediately." He does not speak as we leave the city. His face is a stony mask, and in the storm clouds of his eyes there is a darkness I had not imagined possible. An hour earlier, we were laughing and coming up with new strategies for work. How had everything changed so quickly?

As we reach Versailles, I can hold back no longer. "Georg, we can still do something about this." The car pulls up in front of the apartment building, any notion of working tonight seemingly forgotten. Georg walks me hurriedly to the door, head low. Then, he climbs back inside the car and a moment later is gone.

14

Sunrise comes as it always does over the fields to the east, illuminating the town below in pale yellow like the lights coming up on the set of a play. I cross the bedroom and pick up my dress, which lies where I'd dropped it to the floor the previous evening. The giddy anticipation with which I'd prepared for my date with Georg seems like another lifetime. I see his face, happy one moment and broken the next. He had pinned so much on the peace process, but those dreams are gone now.

I raise my hands to my lips, which are tender and swollen from our kiss. Guilt rises in me. Once could be seen as an accident. But this time I had kissed Georg and it was deliberate, prolonged. I replay the moment in my mind, wondering what might have happened if we had not been interrupted by the fireworks. How can we ever go back from here as though nothing has happened?

Of course, there is no back, I reflect, as I dress. The world Georg and I had known, of quiet evenings working together, had come to an end last night with the issuance of the peace treaty.

Papa had been gone when I'd come into the apartment the previous night. But he is here this morning, and up uncharacteristically early, hunched over his desk. "Papa, the treaty…"

He straightens and turns toward me. His face is gray and dark circles ring his eyes, as though he has not slept at all. "You've heard." His voice is heavy and cracked around the edges. He is nearly as devastated as Georg, I realize. Papa had been cautious about the scope of Wilson's plan, but he'd held out hope for a world that could be put together after the war a bit better somehow. That world seems not to be. He holds up some papers.

"Is that it?" I ask.

He nods. "The official treaty won't be presented to the conference until later this morning, but I received an advance copy by courier." I walk to the desk, lean over his shoulder. "It's a disaster. Millions of marks in reparations. We're losing Alsace-Lorraine and the Sudetenland. It's hard to fathom the country making it through this." I wait for him to offer his usual moment of hope, or attempt to shield me from the harsh reality of what has happened. But he does not. "I should go today and see about booking our passage home."

"No!" I cry. His eyes widen at my outburst. "I mean, the conference isn't over." But my explanation does little to lessen his surprise. I have always complained about having to be in Paris and I can see him trying to comprehend as to my changed demeanor, why I might be upset to be leaving it now.

"My work is done here, darling. There's no reason for us to stay any longer."

"But Georg's work...if we can just offer an alternative proposal. It doesn't have to be this way."

"Captain Richwalder is fooling himself, my dear. It's over." And I know that he is right. So does Georg, I think, remembering how he slumped in such defeat on the ride back from Paris. "So we will be returning to Berlin." His declaration should hardly be a surprise. With the work of the conference largely done, there is no reason to stay.

"I've contacted Greta about reopening the house," Papa adds. I had not thought of the sweet-faced maid in months. With all of our moving about over the years, life sometimes seemed like a movie set, places and people ceasing to exist once we'd left them behind.

He could not have contacted Greta so quickly, I realize now. He must have done so even before the treaty terms were announced. Though he has spent a good deal of his time with the German delegation the past few weeks, his work at the ministry must have given him a strong indication that the end was near and it wasn't good. This explains his troubled looks and his caution that I not become too invested in Georg's work.

Home. The idea prickles at me like a cactus. I knew that sometime this would have to end. Paris has been a buffer between me and the life that awaits. It could not go on forever. But Germany, with the political chaos and rioting, feels dark and dangerous, a country no longer our own. "Will it be safe for you in Berlin, with everything you've written?" I ask, recalling what Ignatz had said months earlier about Papa not using a pseudonym.

"I'm not worried," he replies, stopping somewhere short of answering my question.

Krysia's voice comes back to me: *Now or never.* "Papa…" I lick my lips, preparing to tell him that I'm not going back. "Remember when we spoke of my studying abroad? I'd like to go when we've finished here, perhaps back to London."

"But with the war over, I thought you'd be eager to return."

"It needn't be a formal degree," I offer, retreating. "Perhaps language classes."

"But you can do that in Berlin."

"It would be so much better to study in the native tongue." Unable to lie to him anymore, I drop all pretense. "I need to see a bit of the world. I can't go back. Not now."

"But Stefan…" He stops as he grasps that my fiancé is the very reason I cannot go. I watch as he wrestles with the conflict. Papa is not a young man and his deepest desire is to have his only child settled and taken care of before he is gone. Not just for financial reasons—Uncle Walter would always make sure that I want for nothing. Rather, he wants me to have the companionship he has lacked since my mother died, to be with someone I love. But doesn't he understand that there are worse things than being alone?

"We can stay a few days longer," Papa offers as a concession. "Perhaps a trip to the south."

"No, that's not necessary." If we are going to leave, best to face the inevitable quickly.

"Georg is from Berlin, too, isn't he?" he asks, sidestepping his real question.

I shake my head, looking away. "Hamburg." The cities

are only hours apart by train but it doesn't matter. Once I am back in Berlin and married to Stefan, our separate worlds might as well be on different planets.

"Liebchen," Papa says gently.

I turn back. A single tear runs down his cheek. "Oh, Papa!" I rush to him. I throw my arms around him. Great sobs rack his body, a dry, unfamiliar wheeze. "I won't go. How thoughtless of me to even mention it today...."

He straightens, wiping his eyes. "I'm terribly sorry. It wasn't that at all." Then what? He pulls out a handkerchief and walks to the mirror to compose himself. A moment later, he turns back. "Sometimes we want things that we cannot have. We must accept that." I hold my breath waiting for him to bring up Georg. Should I deny it or tell him the truth, whatever that is? But he is skating just shy of the issue, talking to me in generalities at a more abstract, safe level. "It isn't always possible...."

"But you've always said I must be true to myself," I protest, borrowing his favorite Shakespeare quote. "And that's how you live."

"I try. But it is like the peace conference—sometimes the things that we want and aspire to must coexist within the realm of what is possible." There is a look of longing in his eyes and I want to ask him what he has been forced to compromise. There is a silent gulf between us I have never been able to cross, though, a place in him that for all of our love I cannot reach. I do not press, knowing that he will say no more.

The doorbell rings. He hesitates, not wanting to interrupt our conversation. "That's my car. We can continue this later."

I nod and walk back to my room, peering out the window in the direction of the hotel. *Georg.* I see his face last night, hollow as he read for the first time the draconian terms of the peace treaty, crushing to a pulp everything for which he's worked. I want to go check on him and reassure him. But I suspect he's withdrawn to a place too far and dark for me to reach.

When Papa's car has pulled away, I walk back to the sitting room and cross to the desk, searching for a copy of the peace treaty. Maybe if I can understand it better, I can find a glimmer of hope in the details. Papa has taken the documents with him, but perhaps there is something in the press. I search the desk for *Le Journal,* which I often read after Papa has left it scattered across his desk. But today it is nowhere to be found. He must have taken it with him, as well, in order to digest the treaty coverage.

I walk downstairs to the newsstand at the corner. *"Le Journal,"* I request.

She shakes her head. *"Non."* With news of the treaty, the paper must have sold out quickly. I pick up instead a copy of the *Paris Herald,* curious what the foreign press will have to say. As I pay the seller, she smirks, as though the harsh treaty terms are to be imposed on me personally. Averting my eyes, I carry the paper back up to the apartment. The front-page story carries most of the details I already know from the previous evening. I flip to the inside, searching for more.

At the bottom of the second page, there is a photograph of a beautiful woman that seems oddly placed with the treaty. It is an unrelated story: *Fatal West End Fire,* the headline reads. A massive blaze had broken out at one of the London theaters shortly before showtime. The play had been political in nature and some of the exits had been locked to keep out the protesters. A half-dozen people, including the pictured actress resting in her dressing room before the performance, had been killed.

Papa and I had been to the West End once to see a show before the travel restrictions on Germans had been imposed, an Oscar Wilde play whose title I cannot remember. The century-old theater, with the balconies and ornate carvings around the stage, had been beautiful. But the plush curtains and wooden stage would have made the place a tinderbox, escape from a fire difficult with the narrow aisles and shrouded doorways.

I study the photo again. The woman's large luminescent eyes leap out at me, as familiar as my own. Suddenly it is as if I am looking in a mirror. I scan the caption. The actress was Lucinda Rose, formerly of Berlin. A chill runs up my spine. My mother had been an actress, too, before she had married. But she had died years ago.

My eyes travel from the photograph in the newspaper to the one that sits over the mantelpiece. Though the woman in the paper is older, the heart-shaped face is unmistakably the same. "Oh!" I cry aloud, bringing my hand to my mouth.

There is a noise at the door, footsteps behind me. "I forgot some papers...." Papa's voice is difficult to hear over the roaring in my ears. "Darling, are you...?" He stops midsentence as he leans over my shoulder and sees the newspaper.

I do not look up. "It's her, isn't it?"

I hold up the paper, waiting for the denial. Silence. I turn in time to see his face crumple. His earlier tears had not been about the conference. He had seen the article, taken the newspaper to hide it from me. "Margot, wait..." he calls as I stand and walk to my bedroom, slamming the door behind me.

He raps on my door, then opens it slightly. "Let's talk about this."

"What is there to say? She's my mother, isn't she?"

I wait for him to deny it, to offer some explanation that would make the past ten years something other than a lie. "Yes, she is. Or I should say *was*." His voice cracks on the last word.

"But, Papa, why?"

He sits at the end of the bed, suddenly looking very tired and much older. "I thought it would be easier for you to accept that she had died." Rather than the truth—that she had left us. "When I met your mother she was a rising star of the stage, poised for greatness. I wooed her and convinced her to leave it all for me." A married woman never would have been allowed to continue to act and tour. She would have been expected to choose between the footlights and family.

He continues. "She was always restless, though, and resentful of me for taking the greatness that might have been hers. The story I told you was partially true. She did have the flu and she very nearly died, but when her body healed her spirits didn't. She was morose after that, and said she felt a prisoner." She felt trapped by a husband and baby. *Me.* "She wanted to leave and I couldn't stop her."

So she had left us, whether driven by her depression or something else, I do not know. I picture the elaborate headstone erected in the cemetery in Berlin. It was all a ruse, intended for my benefit—and hers. Better a cherished memory of a mother who had died than hatred for one who had abandoned me. "I planned to tell you when you were old enough." I'm twenty—why isn't that old enough? He continues. "So that way you could make your own decision, maybe even meet her…"

But that opportunity had been taken from me. The article said the show she was in had toured Paris just months earlier. We were in the same city, might have passed each other on the street. If only I had known.

"Did you suspect she would leave?"

But he shakes his head. "Never. I knew she was discontented, but when I pressed her as to what she wanted, she would not say." *Because the thing she wanted was not something you could have given her—freedom.* "I'm not sure I could have stopped her—she was suffocating." Papa had always regarded my mother as a fragile object, one too perfect and beautiful to be his, a prophecy that had proved to be true the day she left.

Could I have done something differently? If I'd been a neater child, with combed hair and clean dresses and good manners, instead of always knocking things over and throwing fits and climbing trees. In an instant I am nine again, reliving the abandonment. But this loss, coupled with re-